Six Days of Christmas

A Heart of Trust

By
Carmellia Chavers

May your holiday season be wonderful! Enjoy!
Carmellia Chavers
1/1/2020

Copyright © Carmellia Chavers 2019
All rights reserved.
ISBN: 978-1-7331204-2-5

2320 Mt. Humphries/OD
Corona CA 92879

Dedication

This book and every future book will be dedicated to two good hearted, down to earth, simple people; my mom, Mrs. Willie Thorpe and my dad, Mr. Oneilous Thorpe. They raised and reared six great children. Although they are both gone, I know they would be proud of my accomplishment. My mom once said, "Although we didn't say it a lot, that didn't mean you all weren't loved." I will always miss my dad's big laugh and baritone singing voice, and my mom's smile and soprano singing voice when she was in the kitchen cooking one of her delicious dinners.

Car

Acknowledgements

I thank God for the gift of imagination He placed inside of me, and the love of *love* He placed in my heart. Thanks to all my friends and family who encouraged me on the long journey to this publication, as well as the people I only just met. Thank you all for always asking, "have you finished your book yet?" Thank you for keeping it in the forefront of my mind. Thank you to the great organizations of *Romance Writers of America, National*, and the *Orange County Chapter* for having such great workshops and conferences where I learned the art and business of writing. I would also like to thank *Romance Slam Jam* for shining a spotlight on African American Romance Writers.

To all of the great romance writers before me, thank you for blazing the trail and sharing your knowledge of writing. Some of those beloved authors are: Jacquelin Thomas, Francis Ray, Rochelle Alers, Maureen Child, Ebony Snoe, Felica Mason, Brenda Jackson, Beverly Jenkins, C.F. Hawthorne, Jane Ann Krentz, Sandra Kitt, Carmen Greene, Donna Hill, Nora Roberts, Jacqueline Diamond, J.M. Jefferies, Samantha James, just to list a few. I could go on, but the list is too long. I have spent many hours reading, enjoying and studying your prose, thank you!

Lastly, a big shout out to Mike and Cherie Johnson of *Extravagant Promises Press, LLC* for encouraging me to sign with their publishing company.

Chapter 1

Elijah Edward Thornton, affectionately known as Eli, stood next to his father half listening as Edward gave him the details of their upcoming trip to Florida.

"Eli are you listening to me son?"

"Yes dad, I'm listening."

His parents were planning on visiting Eli's favorite aunt for Christmas. The two men sipped sparkling grape cider from crystal wine goblets because Eli's sister had just announced she and her new husband, Mitchell, were going to become parents. So, there would be no alcohol this holiday. Sheila Thornton, now Sheila Brennen, stood in their New York apartment next to Mitchell, talking with their mom, Eliza Thornton, affectionately known as Lizzy to their father Edward. Sheila's face was awash with excitement as it had been all day.

Eli loved their family gatherings. The Fourth of July get togethers, birthdays, their parent's anniversary, Thanksgiving, Christmas and New Years were all celebrated as a family. Sadly, over the years his and Sheila's lives had become busier with their careers and finding time to get together had become more difficult. Thanksgiving was usually the holiday when everyone made sure to be available. Before it had always been the four of them; now they were five and in eight months or so, there would be six of them.

Eli knew change was inevitable, but to him it was always unsettling. When Sheila told the family she had met someone, Eli knew this was it... change and he had immediately gone on the defensive. Growing up, he had always looked out for Sheila, been her protector as well as her confidant. His position had been be transferred to someone else and he felt it was a personal loss.

Sheila had found the man whom she wanted to spend the rest of her life and raise a family with. Mitchell was very charming, warm, well-educated and an accomplished, self-made millionaire by age 29. About three years ago, Sheila told Eli and his parents she was going to marry Mitchell, however had changed her mind a few months later. Mitchell did everything but crawl to get her back, even asking Elijah for help. Mitchell had withstood the grueling inquisition from Edward Thornton as to why the engagement to his baby girl had been broken. While Eli took no joy in the torture Mitchell had endured, he also wanted to know the reason. Growing up in the Thornton household, Eli had a feeling he already knew. He had asked Mitchell questions about his intentions toward Sheila.

"She is my heart." Mitchell had replied. He went onto explain he had been an only child and his father, who had not been a part of his life, recently died after a lengthy illness. Sheila had encouraged him to make a connection with his father before he had passed and Mitchell was very grateful for her support.

Edward cleared his throat and frowned at his son who seemed to be distracted. Eli blinked then refocused his attention back to his father.

"I was listening, Dad. You were talking about your upcoming trip to Aunt Gloria's next month and yes, I will be fine. We have a new marketing campaign starting after Christmas and I want to review it over the holidays to get everything sorted out before the team gets back after the New Year."

Eli worked for *DHP Advertising* located in Chicago as an account manager. He and his creative team had contributed to much of DHP's success and would be celebrating his 10th year with the company in January.

Edward exhaled then faced Eli as he laid his hand on his shoulder.

"You know I'm proud of you son and I want you to succeed in life, but you also need a break. There is more to life than work. I did not realize that when you and your sister were growing up."

Eli's mother walked over to where they stood and his father smiled, then kissed her hair. "I was just telling Eli about our trip to Florida over the Christmas holiday but I don't think he was listening."

His mom smiled.

"Do you have any plans, Sweetie?"

Eli frowned. "Mom, I'm thirty-two years old; why do you still call me 'Sweetie?'"

She stepped closer to him, then tenderly kissed his cheek.

"You were a sweet child and now a wonderfully sweet man," his mother said. "I don't care how old you are, you will always be my 'Sweetie.' Someday you're going to make some woman very happy."

Lizzy patted Eli's cheek then rubbed off the lipstick imprint of her lips. The frown on Eli's face faded as he stared at his beautiful, soft spoken mother. She knew just the right words to diffuse his annoyance.

Eli blinked, then cleared his throat.

"I'll probably work. I was just telling Dad we landed this new campaign. There is a lot of prep work I want to get out of the way before the team gets back from their holiday."

His mother raised a perfectly arched brow.

"I wish you had your own company. You work so hard for others. It's time to do it for yourself."

In that instant, Eli smiled at a lovely memory of his maternal grandmother, who always said, "You're not working for anybody but the Lord." Eli had been working on his business plan for the last eight months. Advertising was what he knew and he excelled at it even though advertising was a very competitive business. His mom was right. His father had taught him to always do your best, whether you are working for yourself or others.

"I will Mom," Eli said, smiling at his mother.

"Did you finish your business plan, son?" his father asked.

"Yes sir," Eli replied.

"Good. When you're ready, you should have Mitchell look over it to make sure you've covered all of your bases."

Eli nodded. He smiled as Sheila and Mitchell joined them. "Are you two trying to convince Mr. Workaholic to go to Aunt Gloria's with you?"

Edward chuckled and said, "Eli doesn't want to hang out with us old folks anymore."

Eli placed his hand on his father's shoulder.

"You're not that old, Dad, but close," Eli said with a grin, which elicited laughs from the family.

"Watch it," his dad said with a big smile. "One day, you'll be in my shoes."

"I hope so," Eli said with a grin. He went onto explain to Sheila and Mitchell his plans to work over the holiday on a challenging new project.

"Is Jonah going home for Christmas? I know he has a sister," his mother asked.

Jonah Hill was the front man for the team and soon, Eli hoped to be his business partner. Jonah met with the clients before the team, determining the best way to present a client's product to the public. Eli and Jonah had worked together for three years and he was going to approach Jonah with the business opportunity after this campaign was done.

"Yes ma'am," Eli responded. "He will be going to California for the holidays. As a matter of fact, I am going to go to his place and watch some college football games this weekend."

"Give him our best," his mother said.

"I will. Mom."

Chapter 2

Eli sighed as he looked at the gray Chicago sky through the windshield of his sedan. He was not going to let the day dictate his mood. He was on his way to Jonah's home for a little football and relaxation. Eli wasn't going to think about the morning conversation he had with his mother. Lately, it seemed every family gathering and phone conversation he had with his mother ended with a question about him settling down and starting a family. It wasn't like he didn't ever want to get married, just not right now.

He had apologized for his abruptness to Eliza Thornton during their morning conversation. Eli had cut her off in mid-sentence to let her know he did not want to discuss the subject any longer. He explained to her all he wanted to concentrate on right now was preparing to open his new business.

He rolled his shoulders and tried to physically shrug off the still nagging feelings of guilt. If his dad had heard the way he had talked to his mother, there would be have been hell to pay. Elijah made a mental note to call and apologize again to his mother before he went to bed tonight.

Snow flurries began to stick to the sedan windshield. Eli activated the windshield wipers then stopped at a red light behind a brown compact car. His mind shifted back to his mother's desire to have him married. Looking back at his parent's marriage, he had not seen anything to make him want to have what they shared. He did not remember them ever showing affection for each other.

While they were not affectionate towards one another, he and Sheila knew their parents loved them unconditionally. Sheila was married to a man who openly adored her and was overjoyed during Thanksgivings celebration. His mother's eyes had misted and for the rest of the evening she kept sending him knowing looks. Like "when are you going to give us the same news?" His mother knew he was leery of getting in any close relationship after Phyllis Emery, who he had nearly asked to marry him.

Pushing those thoughts aside, Eli exhaled as the light changed, permitting the cars in front of him to move forward. He made a right turn on a familiar street then made a left turn at the stop sign on his way to Jonah's home. They had planned on hanging out, watch a game or two, eat junk food and try not to talk about work.

Their entire advertising team had been working hard on this last campaign. It was for one of the company's largest accounts. As their boss told them last Monday, they were part of one of the best advertising teams in the industry. Those words were only additional confirmation he and Jonah should be making money for their own company instead of just getting a commission. The commission was good and appreciated, but it would be sweeter if they were doing it for their own company.

Eli thought, who better to go into business with than Jonah? Jonah Hill was a first-rate advertising executive. His ideas were young and innovative; they were 'the future.' When Jonah had an idea, he would stare off into nothingness for what seemed like forever and the results were pure genius. Together, Eli and Jonah had landed some of the largest accounts in the history of *DHP Advertising Agency*.

DHP was a family owned business and the CEO, Donald H. Peters, had made it very clear to all the advertising execs: unless you married into the family, you would never own a piece of the company. In Eli's case that was not going to happen.

He and Jonah traveled a lot. One or both of them were on a plane at least once a month and neither had time for any long-term relationships. Eli thought back to the conversation he and Jonah had on a flight from the state of Washington after a commercial wrap up.

"Hey man, that was an awesome wrap party," Jonah said from the window seat.

"Yeah, we were lucky we didn't miss our plane," Eli replied. "The lead actress really wanted to thank you for giving her a chance in the commercial."

Jonah gave him a faint smile.

"Right—in her bed. I have a feeling she expected me to take her up on her offer. You'd better be glad I didn't tell her you were the one who made the final decision."

Eli laughed then said, "Thanks for sacrificing yourself for a brother. She wasn't my type. What was she doing to you over in that corner by the potted plant anyway?"

Jonah raised his brow.

"Putting her hands and mouth where they didn't belong. You owe me, Eli."

Eli frowned to hide a smile that was threatening his lips as Jonah complained. When he started work at DHP, Elijah had asked everyone to call him Eli instead of addressing him as Mr. Thornton. He wanted everyone to feel comfortable enough to share their thoughts and ideas when they were working on a project. There was a very strict policy among their team: never get personally involved with a client before, during or after a campaign. Eli looked at Jonah's profile and could not help but laugh at the imprint of a pair of perfectly shaped red lips on his jaw.

"Looks like she left you a souvenir," Eli said, with a laugh.

"What?"

"Your cheek."

Eli tapped his own right jaw then tried unsuccessfully to stop smiling. Jonah reached inside his tailored gray suit jacket and took out a gray silk handkerchief, wiped his cheek, then frowned at the offending red stain on the material.

"Man, you let me walk around all this time with a set of red lips on my jaw and didn't say anything?"

Eli chuckled. "Hey, I don't go around staring at your pretty face to make sure it's perfect."

Jonah frowned as he scrubbed his jaw once more.

"You owe me big for this, Eli."

The sound of a car horn brought Eli back to the present. He had decided a year ago to open his own firm with Mitchel reviewing his business and financial plan. He had decided not to take any of their clients with him because he didn't want any drama from DHP. Starting fresh would be scary and challenging. Eli, however, was always up for a good challenge and if he knew Jonah Hill as well as he thought he did, the same went for him. There was only time to stay focused on what was ahead of him. Nothing else.

Eli pulled his midnight blue BMW sedan into an empty parking space in front of Jonah's condominium complex. He grabbed the bag with chips, dip and a six-pack of his favorite brew before getting out of the car. Jonah never bought the beer. Eli knew he preferred wine.

He walked up the three steps to the front door and was about to ring the bell when the door opened. Jonah stood there with a huge smile on his face.

"Hey man, right on time."

They clasped hands and bumped shoulders.

"Were you looking out the window or something?"

"Sort of," he said as he looked back at what Eli knew to be the guest bedroom. "My sister's visiting for the holidays and she caught a cold, so I sent her to bed. Let me take those."

Jonah took the bag and beer then headed for the kitchen as Eli closed the door, then removed his jacket. Although they had known each other for about four years, Elijah had never met Jonah's sister, the elusive Miss Tauri Hill.

Eli hung his jacket in the small closet off the foyer, then noticed a picture on a table to his right and picked it up. He studied the woman who sat smiling as Jonah hugged her from behind, his face next to hers. Her beautiful light brown eyes sparkled as a dazzling smile lit up her perfectly heart shaped face. The two of them looked carefree and loving as they stared into the camera. Eli remembered other pictures Jonah had in his office of his sister but her hair was different. It was much shorter than it was in this picture where cinnamon colored shoulder length curls framed her face.

"She's something else, huh?"

Eli jumped, embarrassed he was caught staring at Tauri's picture. "Oh, yeah. I was just..." he said as he placed the picture back on the table.

"I know. People always do that when they see her pictures. That photo is the newest one," Jonah said.

"When was it taken?"

"Last year, when I went back home for Christmas."

Eli cleared his throat.

"You don't seem to be bothered by..."

Jonah smiled tellingly then said, "...you drooling over my sister's picture?"

Eli cleared his throat again. "Yeah."

Jonah shrugged. "Tauri can take care of herself, believe me. Remember I told you, she raised me after our mom died when I was in junior high."

Eli nodded.

"Tauri had just begun her third year at Spellman when our dad died of a massive heart attack. She transferred to UC Riverside, which was closer to home but against our mom's strong objections."

Eli knew Jonah referred to the University of California.

"When our mom died almost a year later, Tauri became my legal guardian," Jonah added.

Jonah seemed tentative as he walked over to the living room and handed Eli a beer. He picked up the television remote from the coffee table and plopped down on the sofa. Jonah pressed a key on the remote to the 62-inch flat screen LED television, which was mounted over the fireplace, until he found the game they were going to watch. Eli sat next to Jonah and twisted the top off his frosted brew.

Jonah muted the television and continued.

"In my senior year, I was too afraid of life after high school. You know—what everyone expected of me—my parents, Tauri, and myself. Dad had been our biggest supporter and without his presence, I was lost. Things went from bad to worse and I wanted to drop out of school after mom died."

Eli smiled and nodded. Both his parents had been there for him and his sister, but it had been his father who always pushed him to be his best.

Jonah looked at Eli, a lopsided smile on his lips.

"Dad would always say he and mom were behind us one hundred percent in whatever we wanted to do in life, as long as it was for our good. I never asked him how I would know what was for my good. I thought he'd be around forever, you know."

Silence hung in the air between them for a moment as both men stared at the pre-game highlights on the large screen.
Jonah cleared his throat.

"Anyway, I played hooky a few days and liked it. No pressure. I thought Tauri would never find out because she worked a part-time job at night and attended college during the day. We were very fortunate. Our parents had set aside college funds for us both, the house where Tauri now lives had been our grandparents and was mortgage free thanks to our grandfather's frugalness. At our grandfather's passing, life insurance death benefits paid the remaining balance. The spacious two story, five-bedroom house had been bequeathed to our dad and then passed onto me and Tauri."

"Our parents had also bought Tauri a new car as a high school graduation gift. When my mom passed, we did not have many bills except what it took to run the house. Tauri was frugal like our parents and always had money put away for emergencies."

Jonah fondly remembered and was grateful their parents had always supported and pushed them to explore new things. Neither Dwayne nor Felicia Hill had attended college, but they were determined to send both of their children if they so desired. Together with their parent's savings and a trust fund left to he and Tauri by their maternal grandmother, they both were able to attend any college which they applied and were accepted.

Jonah leaned forward and retrieved an open soda from the coffee table then took a drink. He smiled then looked at Eli.

"I didn't know she called my school every other week to see how I was doing."

Eli whistled, then took a drink from his beer.

"What did she do when she found out?"

"I still remember how furious she'd been when I tried to mouth off at her when she confronted me. She threw everything at me she could get her hands on. A lot of them hit dead center mostly because I could not believe what she was doing, so I didn't duck right away. Then she hit me with the 'what would mom and dad think?' speech."

"That was low."

"Yeah, but effective. She wouldn't smile at me for a week. I had to get a part-time job which started right after school and she found time to check all my homework. I had to save all the money I made to get a car and for two years after high school, I had to attend a community college. She said it was to make sure I was serious before she used any of my college fund to send me away to a four-year school."

"Makes sense," Eli said with a nod.

"I still don't know how I managed to get into to Stanford, but I know she took some of her college fund to pay for it."

Eli took another swig of his beer.

"Damn, she was good," Eli said, knowing Jonah's grades had been excellent.

Jonah smiled. "Yeah, and I love her for it."

The pre-game show concluded, Jonah adjusted the volume far below their normal game time level, and they both settled back to watch their opposing teams play.

Chapter 3

Tauri Shamela Hill turned over in her bed in her brother's guest room for the third time, trying to get comfortable. Her nose refused to let air pass through her throat, which was raw, and she had barely been able to swallow the leftover Thanksgiving turkey she'd had for lunch. She was getting sick which was unbelievable since she hardly ever caught a cold. She could not afford to—she had a business to take care of.

"I don't have time for this," she groaned before she turned over again.

The quarter bottle of nighttime cold medicine Tauri found in Jonah's bathroom sat on the nightstand. Jonah would have to go get some more soon. She tried to breathe in through her nose again with no luck.

Tauri had come to spend Thanksgiving with Jonah this year. He had always come to California for the holidays, because she could not get away long enough to spend any quality time with him. She promised to spend four days with him since she had closed the daycare centers the entire long holiday weekend. It was already Saturday and tomorrow she had a late afternoon flight back to California.

Maybe if she rested today, she would feel better tomorrow. Tauri took the rest of the cold medicine and downed the last of her orange juice. Tomorrow, she willed herself to feel a lot better. Tauri laid back on the fluffy pillows, pulled the comforter over her head, and drifted off to some much-needed sleep.

Early Sunday morning, a fit of coughing rocked Tauri fully awake. She sat up in bed until it subsided. Her chest hurt. Her nose was stopped up and her throat felt as if there were rocks inside, causing her to wince every time she swallowed.

A quick knock sounded on the bedroom door and Jonah stuck his head in, "Taur, are you okay?"

"No," she moaned then sneezed.

Tauri sounded pathetic, even to her own ears. She hated being sick. Another sneeze exploded from her already aching body. She cleared her throat and held up her hand when Jonah began to walk into the room.

"And stay away. I don't want to get you sick. What time is it?"

"Almost ten. I figured you didn't feel well enough to go to church."

"Church! It's Sunday morning?"

"Yeah, you looked so peaceful last night, and I knew you needed your sleep."

"Thanks Jonah, but why didn't you go to church?"

"I didn't want to leave you alone," she sniffed, "Thanks, but I would've been okay."

"Did you take all of the cold medicine?"

"Yes." She sniffed again, then sneezed.

"Do you want to go to Urgent Care?"

"No. There are probably more sick people there. I'm staying here. I'm sure I'll be all right."

He stood by the door in what looked like a moment of indecision. Finally, he said, "okay. I'll go get some chicken soup and more cough medicine."

"And tissue," Tauri tried to yell just before another sneeze racked her body.

"Okay, I'll be right back."

All she could do was nod. She threw the covers back and made a trip to the bathroom. When she was finished, Tauri lay back on her pillows, pulled the covers over her, then closed her eyes.

The next thing she knew, a knock sounded again on the bedroom door.

"Taur, are you awake?"

Jonah walked in, carrying a tray laden with steaming hot soup, some crackers, a tall glass of orange juice, a box of tissue and a new bottle of cold medicine with a small plastic dosage cup on top.

He perfectly balanced the tray in one hand while he removed the other items from the nightstand before setting the tray down. In his last year in high school, Tauri had made Jonah get a job as a waiter at a neighborhood restaurant.

"Thanks Jonah. What time is it?"

"Two forty-five"

"Oh Jonah, my plane!"

She threw back the covers and flung her legs over the side of the bed. Tauri stood and was immediately assailed with a bout of dizziness. Her body weaved, and her head began to throb. Jonah quickly griped one of her arms to stabilize her.

"Get back in that bed," Jonah commanded, as he grabbed the covers and patiently waited for her to comply. "I rescheduled."

She tried to raise her brow, but the small action sent another throbbing pain through her temple. She slowly stacked her pillows against the headboard then returned to her place in bed. Jonah quickly continued.

"I think you need another few days to recuperate. Now sit back and eat your soup."

Tauri just sat there and stared at him. She was momentarily stunned by the sharp tone of Jonah's words. The dizziness quickly subsided, and she tried to focus on what he was saying through the throbbing in her temple.

Tauri had not heard Jonah speak to her in such a way in a long time. It was right after her mother's death and at twenty-one she had been named his legal guardian.

She knew back then his words were spoken out of hurt, confusion and maybe a little fear. Now she knew they were spoken out of concern for her. She had vowed to take care of herself better after surviving stage two breast cancer. She was also healing from the heartache she felt when the man she thought loved her had walked away when she needed him most. The latter process was taking longer than she was willing to admit.

Jonah frowned as he helped adjust the pillows behind her back.

"Come on Taur. Co-operate. Let me take care of you for once."

A slow smile formed on Tauri's lips as she settled back and pulled the covers over her lap.

"Now sit up and eat," Jonah told her. "You should call Claire and let her know you're going to take a few more days.

"You mean you didn't do that for me?" she murmured, feigning sarcasm.

"No. I figured I'd take one step at a time."

"I don't know. I have so much to do to get ready for my 'Six Days of Christmas.'

"If I know you Taur, you've already made a laundry list of things I have to do when I go home next month. By then you'll probably have everything ready to go."

She remembered their neighbors and friends offering them whatever help they could after their mom died and when she had gone through the cancer operation then treatment. After these experiences, they had both agreed to give back by helping others whenever they could.

During the six days before Christmas, Tauri baked cookies for the women in a local retirement home, spearheaded a toy drive she and Jonah started for kids at her day care centers and helped serve hot meals at a local homeless shelter. When Jonah had moved to Chicago, he had promised to go home a few days before Christmas to help her. She also knew he always enjoyed doing for others as much as she did.

Tauri knew Jonah's grumbling was done in fun. Jonah protested. Still, she protested.
"Yes, but there are only a few more weeks before..."
"I know Taur," Jonah interrupted and placed the tray over her lap. "I'm sure you have plenty of time but if you don't get better, I don't think you'll be able to do anything."
Tauri relaxed against the pillows, and conceded; "thank you, Jonah. You're right." When he smiled, she added, "And don't get a big head."
Jonah laughed and kissed her on the cheek.
"I'm not in danger of doing that because I always know you'll be around to keep me grounded."
Tauri pushed him away.
"And don't forget it. Now get out. You don't need to get sick."
"Don't worry about me Taur. I have lived here for the last four winters and I am used to it. You are not."
When Jonah closed the door, Tauri tested a spoon full of soup then picked up her cell phone from the nightstand and hit the speed dial number to her preschool director's home phone. Claire Torres answered on the second ring.
"Hola!"
"Hi Claire," Tauri replied trying to sound chipper, but she failed miserably. Her throat hurt but the hot soup felt good going down. She put another spoonful in her mouth and swallowed.
"Tauri is that you?" Claire said, her slight South American accent floating through the receiver.
"Yes," Taura said, sweat beading on her forehead.
"What's wrong? Are you back?"

"No, I'm still in Chicago and I have a really bad cold. Jonah rescheduled my flight," she said, taking a breath of air through her mouth.

"Oh Tauri, you sound horrible. I wish you were here so I could cook you some tortilla soup, extra spicy. It'll knock that cold right out in no time."

"I appreciate that Claire, but you know my stomach can't handle your kind of spicy."

What Claire called spicy was always extra hot to her. Claire had grown up eating roasted jalapenos for dinner.

"You're brave, you can do it."

Tauri chuckled, which was a mistake because it started a coughing spurt.

"Tauri, oh my goodness, are you okay?"

When the coughing subsided, Tauri answered, "No but I will be. Jonah is taking good care of me. I just wanted to know if you can handle things until I return."

"No problem. I don't recall you ever taking a vacation. I'm sure you have more than enough time."

Tauri had placed herself on payroll and made sure her vacation and sick days were calculated the same as her employees. She had accumulated the maximum amount of sick time for the year on the books and at least four weeks of vacation. She was always after Claire to make sure her employees used their time because it was good to take some time for yourself every so often. However, she did not always follow her own advice.

"I would rather spend my time on vacation enjoying myself, not sick," Tauri's complained.

"And when is that gonna happen my friend?" was Claire's reply. "I know you must feel awful, but this is a great opportunity to get some well needed rest. You've worked a lot of long hours lately and that's probably why you're so sick. Your immune system is weak."

Tauri finished her soup as she listened to Claire read her a healthcare riot act. Claire was a registered nurse and Tauri had thanked God for the blessing when she applied for director of her

two childcare centers. Soup finished, she drank some orange juice, then Tauri placed the phone snuggly between her shoulder and ear. She lifted the tray and placed it on the opposite side of the bed, then sank back into the pillows as Claire went on.
"This time you're taking your own advice."

Tauri knew what Claire said was probably right but her thoughts drifted. There had been some very long days and a few longer nights making sure the centers were kept up to code. In addition, there were the quarterly checks to make sure her teachers and attendants kept their credentials updated. She always had the best interest of the children in the forefront of her mind.

Tauri's day care centers were structured as nonprofits and December was the end of their annual contribution campaign. They provided daycare services to struggling parents, single moms as well as single dads who were trying to make life work. With daycare services being so expensive, some mothers would prefer depending upon social services to stay home rather than spend up to half their salaries on childcare. It was especially costly if they had an infant who required special attention the entire time they were at the centers. Through the subsidizing of their fees with grants and donations, the parents or grandparents were able to afford quality, worry free daycare for their children.

Over the past two years the centers had lost two government grants and the usual private contributions were down by almost forty percent. Tauri had wisely built those short falls into the annual budget. She could always cut some of her special projects like new toys, additions to the buildings and extra funds for incidentals, to make sure there was only a slight fee increase for her clients while her employees received their normal pay. If Tauri had to, she would forgo her own salary for a year to make sure her teachers were not short-changed. Each employee had been handpicked. She knew they were all good people who loved what they did and they were worth the salaries they earned.

Tauri had asked for the help of her staff in soliciting new contributors, however with the holidays upon them, this had been challenging. The holidays were always a tough time to solicit new donors but she was determined to meet her annual goal. Ultimately, she envisioned opening an additional center just on the eastside of the city but unfortunately those plans were on hold until the economy picked up.

Tauri refocused on the conversation when Claire said, "You know the little ones are going to ask about you when they come in tomorrow."

"Oh, I know. I really miss them."

"I'll tell them you're not feeling well and will be out a few more days. You know you need a break."

"You've worked just as many hours as I have and..."

"And look who got sick. Tauri, things will be okay here. Please get better. You know we don't need any more of the little ones getting sick."

"I know, I know."

Tauri thought about what Claire said. During the winter months, both centers would have a few children out with colds and someone always had a runny nose.

"Okay Claire. I'll keep in contact with you. Call if you need anything."

"Things here are going to be fine. You take care of yourself and stop worrying."

Tauri knew Claire was right. She could take care of things, but these were her businesses and she had a right to worry.

"Thanks Claire. I know you can handle it. Have a good evening."

"Get some rest, mi amiga. Tell that cutie Jonah, I said 'Hola!'"

"I will."

"Bye."

"Bye."

Tauri drank the rest of the orange juice, then leaned back on the pillows, closed her eyes and breathed a sigh of relief. Her nose had opened a little and she felt slightly better. She had total faith in Claire. Aside from college, she had not been away from her childhood home or the daycare centers for more than a week. She also had a lot of other responsibilities to take care of with the six days of Christmas coming up next month.

Later, the knock on her door was not enough to make her want to open her eyes. Seconds later she heard Jonah's voice.

"Taur?"

Her eyes drifted open. His cute boyish face wore a frown.

"Were you asleep?"

"No, not yet. I talked with Claire to let her know I would be staying until I got better. Thanks for the soup and juice, I feel a little better. Is something wrong?"

A frown on Jonah's forehead became more pronounced.

"About me taking care of you..."

"You're doing fine so far."

"I just received a call from my partner at work and one of us has to go to New York tomorrow morning. He can't go because of a very important morning meeting with a new client he must attend so he asked me to go."

Tauri looked at Jonah and thought how far he had come; from being a smart mouth kid who had not wanted to finish high school, much less go to college. Now, he was a very successful—extremely professional advertising executive. Yet he was concerned about telling her he had have to leave in order to take care of business. She was so proud of him. He had found something he could excel in and loved at the same time.

"Jonah, please don't worry about me. You know I have always taken care of myself. I appreciate what you were trying to do," Tauri said and sniffed.

"I know but I still feel bad about leaving you here alone."

"When are you coming back?"

"As far as I know, Wednesday maybe Thursday. I'll have to assess the situation when I get there."

Tauri pulled her bottom lip between her teeth to hide her smile as her eyes misted. What a difference, if only mom and dad could see him now. Tauri had often wondered what her parents would think of the man Jonah had become.

"Taur? Taur, are you alright?" Jonah said, moving closer to the bed.

She cleared her throat.

"Yes, yes, I'm fine. What day did you reschedule my flight?"

"I had it changed to an open ticket. I printed out the confirmation and it's on the desk in my office."

"Good. I'll be fine. Go on to your meeting."

Jonah stood and stared at her. She smiled the best smile she could manage. Jonah exhaled, then walked over and kissed her on the forehead.

"Thanks, Taur. I will make it up to you. I promise."

"No problem. Please don't worry. You need to take care of business. Go let them know who is in charge. I'll be fine."

Later that evening, Jonah had brought her more soup along with cold medicine. Tauri vaguely remembered Jonah kissing her goodbye the next morning. When she woke up at twelve forty-five that afternoon, she could barely breathe. Her chest hurt. She lifted the cold medicine and read the label. 'For coughing, sneezing and headaches' but not for congestion or body aches.

That explains why she could not breathe. Jonah was gone so she had to go to the drug store and get something to help her get the rest she needed.

She got up slowly and went to the bathroom to take care of her morning needs, thankful she had taken a shower last night. She dressed in a pair of jeans, t-shirt, and tennis shoes. The clothes she had brought with her from California were no match for this Chicago cold, windy weather. She went into her brother's room, looked through his well-organized bureau drawers until she found one of his thick sweatshirts. Then she looked in his closet which was organized by colors and category. Tauri shook her head; she had created a monster.

She grabbed one of his heavy red jackets with Stanford across the back and picked up the keys to his second vehicle, a silver SUV he told her she could drive while she was in town. It was equipped with a navigational system and programmed so if she were ever lost, all she had to do was hit the display labeled "*Home*" and it would direct her back to the condo.

On the way out of the door, she passed a mirror hanging in the foyer. Tauri cringed at the unsightly mass of tangled hair on her head. She went back into Jonah's bedroom and grabbed a red and black knit cap. She was so glad no one in this town knew her but her brother. She climbed gingerly into the silver monster and push "*Pharmacy*" on the navigational system. The firm feminine voice instructed her to please drive the highlighted route.

Eli was expecting a call from Jonah any minute. He was anxious to learn about the progress of the commercial in New York. He and Jonah agreed he was the best person to attend this meeting since it was his brainchild from the beginning. If anyone could handle difficult decisions or challenging problems, it was Jonah.

As he waited for Jonah's call, Eli looked down at the notes his secretary, Iris, had given him from the initial morning meeting he had with their newest client. Overall, he thought the meeting had gone very well and as such, their first meeting was only the preliminary part of the creative process. The very efficient vice president of *Green Clark's Recycling Company* had given him an idea of their president's expectations and vision. Taking this information into consideration, he would get the ball rolling.

The second meeting was scheduled for next week when Jonah could be in attendance. Along with their team, the creative juices would flow propelling them forward to another winning campaign. "Yeah, the profits would again benefit someone else." Eli thought. But it would be only for a little while longer. He had already talked to D.H. Peters, the CEO, about his impending departure. Peters looked as if he had expected it, asking only that Eli and his team, work with the next client to see the project through to completion before he left. Eli agreed. He did not want any bad blood between himself and D.H. Mr. Peters could potentially make things very difficult for him and his new business if he left on bad terms. Eli would tell his team of his departure after the campaign was done.

The ringing phone on Eli's desk brought him out of his thought process. He picked up the handset.

"Thornton."

"Hey man," Jonah said cheerfully on the other end of the line.

"How did the meeting go?" Eli inquired.

"Well, you were partially right on the ideas surrounding the commercial. They aren't easily transferred from paper to action and it might take a minute."

"Yeah. After I called you, I ran the process through over and over and knew it was a hands-on thing. I thought it would make a better impression if we were there for the entire process."

"Now that I am here, I agree."

"Yeah, I noticed you were reluctant about this trip. Would you mind telling me why?"

Jonah was a man on a mission. A mission to excel in this business of advertising so he was always eager to go when and where he was asked. However, when they spoke the night before, Eli had to almost convince Jonah he would be the best person to send to New York.

Jonah was quiet for a minute. He exhaled.

"It's my sister, man.

Eli, growing concerned asked, "I thought she was supposed to go back to California yesterday. Is everything okay over there?"

"She's not back in Cali. Her cold got worse, so I cancelled her flight. She was able to make arrangements at work so she could to take a few days off to recover."

"Sorry to hear that. You made sure she has everything she needs, right?"

"Yeah..."

"But," Eli prompted.

"She's sick and this time I promised to take care of her. She's been taking care of everybody else but she deserves to be cared for too."

"From what you've told me about your sister, she doesn't play tit for tat."

"No, she would never do that, but I always feel like I should pay her back in some way."

"I feel there's something you want to ask me and I'm not sure I'm going to like it."

Jonah sighed, "I hate to ask, Eli, but when you head home today, could you possibly stop by and check in on her?"

Eli's heart rate increased at the prospect of finally meeting the beautiful Tauri Hill face to face.

"How is she going to feel about a stranger stopping by to check on her?"

"I've told her all about you, so she knows about our close working relationship and I'll call to give her a heads up. I'd feel better, man, if you could just make sure."

When Eli didn't respond, Jonah said, "I'll spring for the beer at the Super Bowl party, have the guys over at my place instead of yours, spring for all snacks, AND even give you a three-point spread."

Eli smiled. Jonah was the only person who stood with his team, the "underdog." His team had not been in the Superbowl for eleven years and he was sure they were going to win the game.

If Eli's team won, he would buy the beer next time. Jonah's offer was serious because he always made a point of never buying beer for anyone. Eli knew he was going to say 'yes,' because now he was going to meet the woman who helped make Jonah Hill who he was.

Chapter 4

On his lunch hour, Eli parked his midnight blue, BMW sedan in an empty slot near the entrance of the grocery store a block away from Jonah's condo. A SUV of the same make, model and color as Jonah's was parked in the next space. He decided to pick up a few things before he stopped by Jonah's just in case Tauri did not feel up to cooking.

Eli had planned on working a little late tonight, so he thought he would visit Jonah's sister now rather than stopping by later this evening.

He climbed out of his car and pulled up the collar on his overcoat to help shield his neck from the famous icy Chicago wind. The weather report said it would be in the low thirties today and low twenties by tonight. It felt like the low twenties already with the heavy gray sky showing a definite sign of snow.

Eli entered the store and picked up a red plastic shopping basket. He walked down the aisle marked "*Noodles*" on the overhead isle sign. He found the kind he wanted and placed them in his basket. He turned around when he heard someone sneeze as a can of chicken soup fell to the floor, rolled over, stopping at the toes of Eli's polished black boots. Automatically, he bent over and scooped it up.

"Bless you," Eli said to no one in particular.

When he straightened and found himself staring at a person wearing what he thought was Jonah's Stanford jacket and cap. The persons face was deeply buried in a mound of facial tissue.

The jacket looked a few sizes too big; in fact, it looked like it swallowed the person whole. Could this possibly be Jonah's sister?

At that moment, the woman held her head up and said "Thank you..."

Another sneeze followed then continued—four in all, before ceasing. Tired brown eyes captured Eli's dark ones as he lifted the can in her direction.

Instantly, he knew these were the same pair of eyes that stared back at him from the picture of Jonah and his sister. Except these eyes were weary, red and filled with some other emotion he couldn't quite put his finger on before they looked away.

"Thank you," she said again, sniffed, took the can and put it in her shopping cart.

"Excuse me. Is your name Tauri? Tauri Hill?" Eli asked.

She stopped then slowly turned to face him again.

"I'm sorry, do I know you?"

Her eyes slowly traveled over his face, then down his body. He did not think he had ever been examined so thoroughly and was momentarily speechless.

"My name is Elijah Thornton."

He reached in his back pocket and pulled out his wallet. He pulled out his license and showed it to Tauri. She examined the picture on his Illinois state driver's license and nodded. Eli reinserted his ID then returned the wallet to his back pocket.

"I thought that looked like Jonah's SUV outside. I work closely with your brother."

Tauri continued to stare at him.

"Jonah told me you were sick," Eli said.

A frown formed beneath the brim of the knit cap. She looked as if she were trying to hold on to what he was saying.

"I'm sorry, Mr.....?"

"Thornton. Elijah Thornton but everybody calls me Eli."

"Mr. Thornton."

"Eli."

"OK, Eli." Recognition flashed in her eyes.

"Jonah speaks of you often. It is nice to finally meet you. I would shake your hand, but I don't want to pass on whatever this is I've contracted."

"Nice to finally meet you also. Jonah told me you were in town. He was supposed to call you...about me...stopping by the condo.

He asked me to look in on you on my way home to see if you needed anything."

"That was nice of him to do so but entirely unnecessary. I am fine," she told Eli, then sniffed and coughed.

Eli smiled as he looked in the grocery cart she was leaning on, as if she needed the support.

"I see. So, you won't need that cold medicine or that orange juice or that can of soup?" he said pointing toward the items in the cart.

Tauri frowned as she followed his gaze down into the cart. She winced as if the action caused her pain.

"I meant I was fine as in I can take care of myself."

"From what Jonah has told me, I'm sure you're most capable of doing just that, but it never hurts to have a little help."

"Look, Mr. Thornton."

"Eli."

"Eli, I appreciate your concern." Her breath sounded labored.

"But I'm fine and have always taken care of myself and I am going to continue to do so..."

Her sentence was cut short by a long string of coughs. Eli went over to her and put one arm around her shoulder. When the coughing stopped, Tauri looked up at him.

"Excuse me. I didn't mean to cough all over you."

"Don't worry. I have had my flu shot this year. Have you?"

"Yes."

"Maybe you're so independent because you're from California

and unfamiliar with how brutal Chicago winters can be."

Her lips curved slightly at the corners. Still holding her to his side, Eli looked down into those honey brown eyes and almost forgot what he was going to say.

"Look, why don't we do this? Just so I won't feel like I let Jonah down. Why don't I follow you home," he said, but when she sent him a startled look, he quickly continued, "just to make sure you get there okay."

When she looked like she was going to object, he added, "We do not want to worry Jonah, this project is pretty important to him. It needs his full attention while he is in New York. He knew if he asked me to look in on you, he wouldn't have anything to worry about back here."

Eli noticed Tauri relax just a little. At least the frown was gone and that seemed to do it.

"All right," she sighed. "I just need to get some orange and grape juice and …"

"You already have the orange juice," he said nodding towards her cart. "And I'll get the grape juice on my way to the checkout. Do you need anything else?"

"No, I think that will do it."

She started to push the cart again, but Eli protested.

"No, I'll get those. Just go get in the SUV, turn on the heat and wait for me. It shouldn't take long."

She wiped her nose and said, "Okay."

She reached into the jacket pocket and gingerly handed him a bill.

He leaned over close to her ear and spoke firmly.

"I'll get it."

Fully expecting her to argue, Eli gave her a stern look. She then nodded once and slowly slipped the bill back in the jacket pocket. Eli wanted to help her to the car, but he somehow knew Miss Tauri Hill would not have appreciated it. She did not have far to walk to the SUV with the tell-tale *'Advertisers Advertise'* framing the license plate.

He stood and watched Tauri as she ambled her way through the front door of the grocery store.

Eli felt sorry for her because she clearly didn't feel well. He was very close to picking her up and carrying her to his car, taking her back to Jonah's place then putting her straight to bed. In her condition, she should not out in this weather.

As he took her cart and went back to grab more orange and grape juice, his frustration began to rise. He was upset with himself for insisting that Jonah go to New York to see this project through. If he had gone himself, Tauri would not be alone trying to take care of herself. As he mulled this over in his mind, he made a detour to the produce section to gather ingredients for his mother's homemade chicken soup.

Tauri sat behind the wheel of Jonah's truck wondering why she was out in this weather. Her chest and head hurt. She could not breathe through her nose and she was so tired. Why had she left her things in that cart? She should have taken what she had chosen to the checkout and be on her way back. Instead, she was waiting for Jonah's clean-shaven, handsome co-worker.

While Tauri had spoken with Iris, Jonah's secretary on many occasions she had never met her. This was the first time she had ever personally met any of Jonah's business associates, especially the one he talked about all the time. And of course, she now looked like the abominable snowman's sister. She signed and thought about how Eli was nice on the eyes considering hers were red and puffy. The way he had stared at her—his charcoal black eyes seemed to look past her usual defenses. He was sharp. He had already figured out her Achilles' heel was Jonah.

"Oh, he was gorgeous," she groaned.

She tugged Jonah's knit cap further down on her head. She then touched his oversized jacket which was zipped up to her chin and knew she looked a site. Again, she groaned and leaned back on the headrest. How did he even recognize her?

Tauri jumped at the sound of a knock on the driver's side of the window. She pressed the automatic window control button. Eli's perfect lips parted and flashed a white toothy smile.

"I'm sorry if I startled you." A frown formed over those beautiful intense eyes, "Are you going to make it?"

Tauri nodded.

"Do you know your way back?" he asked.

"No, but she does," Tauri said pointing to the GPS.

Eli chuckled, a deep rich sound that sent a pleasant shiver through her entire body. His smile made her want to touch his handsome face. She blinked then nodded again.

"Okay."

Eli walked around the car parked in the next space and climbed in the driver's side. Tauri hit the automatic driver's side window control again and the window moved back into place. Eli backed out far enough so she could back out in front of him. She looked in her side mirror at him as he waited. She pushed 'Home' on the navigational system and put the SUV in gear. Again, looking in her rearview mirror she exhaled. She was *definitely* in trouble.

When they arrived at Jonah's condo, Tauri parked in the garage, let herself inside, opened the door, and waited for Eli to park and grab the groceries.

"Go lie down," Eli told her as he came in and closed the door with his foot.

"I need to take some cold medicine and eat something and..."

After putting the bags in the kitchen, Eli crossed over to her. He placed his hands on both of her arms.

"Tauri, I'll take care of all that. What I need you to do is..." he began as he unzipped her jacket, "lie down on the sofa for a minute. I'll get your medicine first then make you some homemade soup. It won't take long. Is that okay?" He removed the jacket and tossed it on a nearby chair.

"You don't have to."

Eli stared into those determined eyes.

"But I want to."

Under any other circumstances, he would be tempted to enjoy challenging her, but he could clearly see Tauri didn't know the meaning of asking for help, even when she was ill.

"Let me take care of you, Tauri."

Hmmm, coincidentally Jonah had told her the same thing yesterday. Her extraordinary eyes widened slightly, then Tauri looked down as if trying to come to a decision.

Eli added for impact; "for Jonah's sake?"

Finally, she nodded. Not completely sure, she said, "but you still don't have to."

Eli took her arm and guided her over to the sofa.

"Sit."

She complied.

"I'll be right back."

Eli went into Jonah's room then came out with a large comforter and a pillow.

"Okay Tauri, here you are."

He put the pillow down against one arm of the sofa then gently pushed her down. When she put her feet up on the sofa, he removed her shoes then covered her with the comforter. She looked up at him, still wearing her brother's cap. She looked so vulnerable and so damn cute. He almost smiled but he was sure it would only agitate her a little more. He wanted to do whatever it took to make her feel better.

"I'll be right back."

Tauri wanted to continue her protest but the energy she needed was nowhere to be found. Tauri was thankful she had the strength to walk up the four steps from the garage then make it to the sofa. She closed her eyes. She was so tired.

A strong soft voice called to Tauri through the fog that clouded her head.

"Hold up," Eli told her. "Don't go to sleep just yet. First you take your medicine and drink some juice." She sat up slowly. Eli sat in front of her on Josh's sturdy hard wood coffee table and spooned the cough syrup into her mouth then helped her drink a good portion of orange juice.

"Good. Okay. Now you can take a nap while I fix you something to eat. Okay?"

She nodded.

"Okay."

Satisfied, he turned to walk away.

"Eli."

His name came out broken; she cleared her throat.

"I'm sorry. Excuse me."

He stared down at her with those beautiful eyes.

"Thank you, Eli."

"No problem. My pleasure."

She could see in his eyes that he was telling her the truth. He turned and went back into the kitchen. Tauri took a deep breath, happy her nose was clear for the moment then sank her head into the soft fluffy pillow, surrendering to the sleep she knew her body needed.

Eli had only planned on stopping by during his lunch hour to check on Tauri. After seeing her in this condition, he felt compelled to do whatever he could to nurse her back to health. He removed his overcoat and suit jacket then rolled his shirt sleeves up to his elbows. He washed his hands in the sink then removed the groceries from the bags before looking in the cabinets for a big pot.

Eli looked at the clock on the microwave above the stove and calculated how long it would take to prepare the soup. Over the years he had made the Thornton family chicken soup recipe his own by adding a dash of cayenne pepper. A cold did not stand a chance. His mother had tasted it and approved after a glass and a half of water. He would not be back at work by two o'clock, perhaps four at the earliest. One look at his watch and he knew that would not work. His decision was made.

Eli pulled out his cell and punched the speed dial for his office. Iris Cameron, his personal secretary picked up on the first ring. "DHP Advertising," her soft voice resonated in a professional tone.

She had been a godsend and was the one responsible for bringing him and Jonah together. She had seen something in Jonah Hill, a new hire right out of college and told Eli he should draft him onto his team. Iris thought Jonah needed someone to help him navigate through the world of advertising and knew Eli was the right person for the job.

Iris had been in the advertising business for over twenty-five years and knew the ins and outs of the industry well. She had teenaged kids—one a freshman in college and a daughter graduating high school in the spring. Her husband, Phillip, adored her. He had always said she was his life preserver.

"Hello, Iris," he said in a quiet voice looking over his shoulder to see if Tauri seemed bothered.

"Hi, Elijah," He never had to identify himself. Iris listened intently and immediately recognized his voice. She also was the only one, besides his mother, who called him Elijah.

He smiled. "I'm not coming back to the office today; you can send any important matters to my tablet. Jonah should be calling in later this afternoon. Just let him know I'm out and either transfer the call or have him call me."

He held the phone between his ear and his shoulder as he washed the chicken breast.

"Will do, Elijah," she said paused. "Is everything all right?"

Eli knew she could not resist her mothering instinct.

"Yes, just taking care of some personal business."

"Is there anything I can do?"

Eli looked through the cabinets and found a pot that would be perfect for his soup.

"I don't think so, but I'll let you know if I need anything." He rinsed the pot, added water then set it on the stove and turned on the burner.

"You do that."

He smiled and he knew she meant it.

"I will, I promise. Thanks, Iris. I'll see you in the morning."

He took a cutting board and a knife from the draining tray next to the sink and began to cut the chicken into bite size pieces.

The next call Eli placed was to his doctor, Dr. Leonard Lewis who was a good friend as well as Eli's personal physician. Leo had asked the firm to do some advertising when he moved into the professional plaza near Jonah's home. He and Leo had hit it off right away. When open enrollment came around, Eli decided to make Leo his primary physician.

"Thank you for calling Lewis Medical. May I help you?"

"Good afternoon, Hope. This is Eli Thornton. How are you today?"

"Hello, Mr. Thornton. Well and yourself?"

"Fine thanks. Is Leo available?" Eli asked, hoping he was.

"Hold one minute and I'll check."

Seconds later, she came back on the line.

"Mr. Thornton, he's between patients so I'll put you through. Nice talking to you."

"Thanks Hope. Same here and have a good day."

Moments later, Dr. Lewis's deep voice boomed, "hey man, you're not calling to cancel Sunday, are you?"

Leo sounded hurt. He loved his time with the boys watching the game, eating nachos and talking trash. Before Eli could answer Leo said, "oh don't tell me you've caught this flu bug that's going around."

"No on both points but I have a...friend, who is visiting from out of town, who may have the flu bug."

"Does this friend have a personal physician?"

"I'm not sure. I'll have to ask."

Eli dumped the chicken pieces into the boiling water then washed the cutting board.

"But you want some answers right now?"

"Yeah, I do."

Eli began to wash and chop up the other ingredients for the soup.

"Can you get her to come in?"

Eli didn't answer.

"Eli?"

"How did you know it was a female?"

Leo chuckled, answering; "a wild guess. I think I have an opening tomorrow morning around nine thirty. Can you check with your friend to see if that's okay and if so, call back and leave her name up front with Hope?"

"All right. Thanks, Leo."

"Okay. I'll look forward to seeing you in the morning. Bye."

"Bye."

Eli ended the call, added the vegetables and seasoning to the soup while formulating a plan to convince Tauri to see Leo. Jonah had not warned him his sister would be this much of a challenge. He smiled. Her strong will intrigued him as well as challenged him. She had spunk even when she was sick.

Chapter 5

When the soup was ready, Eli looked over at Tauri as she slept on the sofa still wearing Jonah's knit cap pulled down snuggly over her head. She looked young and defenseless with her thick lashes curled up against her caramel brown skin. For some reason he wanted to take care of her and not as a favor to Jonah. Something in her eyes, if only for a second, had reached out to him. It flashed so quickly he had almost missed it.

He looked through the cabinets in the kitchen in search of a tray or something to carry the food on. Finding one in the corner, he noticed some rum left over from one of his and Jonah's sports get-togethers. He would see if she would try it later with some juice. He ladled the steaming hot soup into a huge bowl setting it on a plate. He took the tray over and placed it on the coffee table. Then returned to the kitchen and poured a glass of orange juice. He kneeled beside the sofa and shook Tauri gently.

"Tauri. Tauri, wake up. You need to eat something. Hun, wake up."

Her eyes opened slowly.

"Umm."

A frown formed on her beautiful brow.

"Eli?"

"Yes," he said with a smile. "You have to eat. Come on, sit up."

Tauri slowly came to her senses. Jonah's friend and co-worker was still there. Now he was standing—no, kneeling next to her, looking at her with those gorgeous dark eyes telling her she needed to eat. Through a stuffy nose she could just smell a hint of his alluring aftershave and something that smelled like chicken soup.

Tauri looked down at the steaming hot bowl of soup and smiled.

"Oh, thank you. It looks good. I wish I could smell more."

Eli was surprised how his stomach clenched when she smiled. Eli did not think her smile would be something he was waiting to see. It did not quite light up her face because her eyes looked tired and weak. She seemed really sick and he had to get her into see Leo first thing in the morning.

Eli sat on the coffee table in front of Tauri as she slowly propped herself up on the pillow. He picked up the soup and the spoon. He took a hearty spoonful, blew it, then he put it to her mouth.

"Try this."

Tauri was pleasantly surprised that he was spoon-feeding her. Not to mention he had blown on it as if she were one of the kids in one of her day care centers. He was even frowning at her. Who is this man?

"Open," he demanded.

She wanted to tell him not to tell her what to do but she did not have the strength. She had not eaten anything since last night and seeing the streetlights visible through the living window, she knew it was already evening. She looked back at the frowning Eli, then opened her mouth.

The soup was warm with plenty of noodles, lots of chicken and an assortment of vegetables. She wished she could taste it. Instantly, her stomach welcomed the food.

He raised another spoonful to her mouth. After a few more, he put the glass of orange juice to her lips. The cool liquid felt good on her raw throat.

"Thank you," she said, after taking another big swallow of juice.

He smiled and continued to spoon the remainder of the soup into her mouth. When the bowl was empty, he gave her more juice but this time she took the glass.

"Would you like more soup?"

"No, thank you," she said clearing her throat. "I just want to sleep."

"That's good, you need it, but we need to talk about something first."

Tauri grabbed a tissue from a nearby facial tissue box just before a sneeze racked through her body. After blowing her nose a few times, Tauri looked again at Eli.

"Excuse me. What were you saying?"

"Bless you. We need to get you to a doctor," Eli told her, smiling as he spoke.

"I told you. I already took the flu shot. I should be fine in a couple of days," she said and coughed.

"I know you had the shot, but I want to make sure it isn't something more severe. It could turn into pneumonia, you know."

Tauri frowned as she looked at him.

"Come on Eli, pneumonia? I doubt I have pneumonia."

"How do you know? Have you ever had it before?"

That got her. She did not reply.

"I made and appointment tomorrow for 9:30AM —no waiting."

Tauri stared at this man who barged into her life not even five hours ago. He had made her soup and made sure she ate it. Now, he had also made her a doctor's appointment and was trying to convince her to go. Again, he was trying to tell her what to do. Tauri and Jonah had been on their own since she was twenty-one. She had made sure he finished high school then college while getting her BA in Business Administration and an AA in Early Childhood Development. It had been very difficult, but she and Jonah had done it. They had been encouraged and received help from friends, her Aunt Ellie and Uncle John. No one had taken care of her this well since her bout with cancer.

The soup had given her a little strength. She sat up straighter on the sofa under the warm comforter, lifted her chin and said, "why don't you just order me to go! It seems to be your thing."

Eli could feel heat rising-up on the back of his neck then climbing to his face. There was a little bit of embarrassment, but he quickly replaced it with a small amount of firmness.

"Look, Tauri, I apologize for that. I have a younger sister who was also very stubborn. When my mom and dad went out, I was the babysitter and she would always try me every chance she got; especially at dinnertime."

He shrugged his wide shoulders.

"And it never worked. I pretty much got my way in the end. In addition, you need to get a doctor to check you out. Jonah asked me to look after you, but he didn't tell me you would be this difficult."

"I don't think I'm being difficult," Tauri pouted. "I was just questioning your diagnosis of my impending pneumonia," she said and wiped her nose.

Eli still sat in front of her on the coffee table and took both of her hands in his. Her eyes went instantly to their joined hands.

"Look Tauri." He waited until her eyes moved to his face.

"I know we haven't known each other very long," he said with a smile. "Man, we haven't even known each other an entire day but I care about Jonah and he cares about you. I want to make sure I do the best job I can."

Tauri looked at him for a long moment, a strange feeling started a reaction to the emotion in his voice. Her eyes narrowed.

"It's not just Jonah you're concerned with is it?"

Eli held her gaze then sighed, "no—no, my maternal grandmother died from a severe case of pneumonia. It started as a common cold so my mom did what I'm doing—soup, juice, cough medicine and plenty of rest. When my 'Grand,' who did not like doctors and didn't improve, my mom bullied her into going to the doctor. She died a week later."

Tauri did't know why but she pulled one hand from his grasp then placed it on his rigid jaw. The hurt she saw in his eyes touched her heart.

"I'm so sorry, Eli. You cared for her very much."

It was more of a statement than a question.

Eli covered her hand on his face with his own. For a moment, they did not say anything. He broke eye contact and swallowed the lump in his throat, then nodded. He closed his eyes and mentally pushed back the memory of his Grand's death. Eli and his family had countless happy memories of Grand that he himself would keep deep within his heart forever.

When Eli opened his eyes, Tauri no longer saw the raw pain that almost broke her heart. In its place was the softness and concern he had displayed earlier.

"Okay, Eli," she conceded. "I'll go to the appointment."

A slow smile found its way to his lips as well as his eyes. He moved her hand from his cheek then kissed the palm. It was not so much of a kiss but a soft caress. A chill raced from her hand, up her arm and quickly made it down her spine. She visibly shook.

"See, you've already caught a chill."

He pushed her softly back down on the sofa and tucked her in, snuggly, under the comforter. When she only stared at him, he asked, "it's still early would you like to go back in the bedroom or stay on the sofa a little while longer?"

She smiled back, and answered, "no this is fine."

Tauri snuggled into the pillow, closed her eyes and thought as she let sleep overtake her again. *'Who is this Elijah Thornton?'* She knew she could not get used to the attention, but it felt good to have someone else take care of her.

When Tauri awoke the next morning, she knew this was not just a cold. She gingerly sat up on the side of the bed. Her head hurt so bad the room seemed to spin when she tried to stand. Her body ached. She felt awful and was glad she had taken a shower just after Eli had left the night before.

She had to get dressed. Eli would be there soon. She managed to get into the bathroom then dress in a pair of loose-fitting jeans, a t-shirt and sweatshirt. She grabbed her purse along with the same knit cap she had worn the day before. She did not even want to know what her hair looked like. Then she slowly made her way to the living room, sat on the sofa and waited for Eli.

Eli arrived at Jonah's condo thirty minutes later. They had plenty of time and he hoped she was ready. The morning traffic was light, but it could have its surprises.

He rang the doorbell, but no one answered. He knocked. Still no answer. He used the key Jonah had given him the last time he had to go out of town. Eli once needed to let a maintenance man in to fix Jonah's air conditioner during one of the hottest weeks of the summer.

Eli eased the door open. He walked into the small foyer, calling as he walked toward the living room.

"Tauri. Tauri? We need to get going."

When he came around the corner, he saw her. Tauri lay asleep on the sofa. He went over and crouched down. She did not look as peaceful as she had yesterday. Just then, her brow wrinkled. When he touched her forehead, an alarm went off inside him. She was burning up. Eli grabbed the same jacket she had worn the day before from a nearby chair.

"Tauri, sweetie."

"Umm?"

"Tauri, come on. Wake up."

He pulled her to a sitting position.

"Eli?"

"Yes, Hun, we have to go. You're burning up."

"Eli, I don't feel well."

She looked so helpless.

"I know. Come on—let me get you into this jacket. When we see Leo, he'll make you feel better."

He put Jonah's jacket on her and zipped it up.

"Leo's going to make me feel better?"

He stared at her eyes. They looked hazy and weak.

"Yes," he consoled her.

"Okay."

He picked her up and started toward the door. Tauri laid her head lazily on his shoulder. As they reached the door, she softly said, "Eli, my purse."

He turned back to the sofa, saw the small black bag on the coffee table, walked back over and picked it up. After Eli closed and locked the front door, he helped Tauri to his vehicle and placed her on the front passenger seat

He fastened her seat belt and ran around to the driver's side, hopped in, and started the engine.

"It should be warm pretty soon." He turned the heat on the highest setting so she would not become chilled.

Thank God Leo's office was only a few blocks away. Eli prayed the traffic remained light. Tauri leaned her head back on the seat and closed her eyes. He glanced at her every so often to see how she was doing. When he stopped at a red light, he touched her forehead again.

"Damn," he whispered.

'I should have wrapped her in the comforter.'

He didn't have much experience with fevers, but he didn't like this one bit. His heart raced in his chest. Ten minutes later Eli turned into the medical complex where his friend, Dr. Leonard Lewis, practiced medicine. He pulled up and parked in a space close to the front door. He hurried around to the passenger side and opened the door.

"Sweetheart, we're here."

When she opened her eyes, she looked distressed.

"You are very sick, Tauri."

"We're going to see Leo," she swooned. "He'll give me something for my headache?"

"Yes, he will."

Tauri reached up and smoothed the frown from his brow.

"That's better," she said in a no-nonsense tone.

"We'd better get you inside."

She nodded.

"Here; take your purse."

When he reached under her legs to pick her up, Tauri offered a feeble protest.

"Eli, you don't have to carry me."

"Yes, I do. Now be still and be quiet," he ordered softly.

"Eli, you need to stop ordering me around."

"If you would do what I ask, I wouldn't have to."

Tauri clutched her purse in one hand and wrapped the other hand feebly around his neck. Eli picked her up and kicked the car door closed behind them. She laid her head on his shoulder.

When Eli walked into the office, the receptionist greeted him cheerfully, "good morning, Mr. Thornton. Come on—follow me."

"Good morning, Hope. Which room?"

"This way. Number 10, down the hall on your right."

Eli ignored the curious on lookers as he followed Hope through the waiting room.

She handed him a clipboard full of papers.

"Here take these and fill them out. I'll get Doctor Lewis."

"Thanks."

Eli was grateful they did not have to wait in the waiting area. He carried Tauri through a short hallway and into Room 10. The door was open. He walked in, placed her on the white paper covered table then turned and closed the door.

He read the questions on the forms to Tauri and filled out enough information he hoped would satisfy the receptionist. He stood then walked to the door. There was a rapid knock then the door opened. Eli quickly stepped back.

A cheery round faced African American young woman, dressed in purple scrubs, came in.

"Hi Mr. Thornton. How are you?"

"I'm fine, Rachel. It's my friend here that I'm concerned about."

"Oh, let me see those."

She took the clipboard from Eli. After a glance at the forms, she asked, "Miss Hill? Any relation to Jonah Hill?"

"His sister," Eli said, then made introductions. "Rachel Donovan, this is Miss Tauri Hill."

The two women smiled at each other.

Eli continued; "she looks like she has a real nasty cold, but I suspect there's something more."

Not having the energy to dispute him, Tauri closed her eyes and tried to relax on the table.

"Well, I'll be sure to let the doctor know. In the meantime, let me take your vitals and go over the forms to make sure we have everything we need. Mr. Thornton, if you could please wait up front in the reception area. I will come out and get you after the doctor has finished his examination. Tauri opened her eyes,

"Can he please stay?"

Rachel looked from Tauri to Eli.

"Okay, but the doctor might insist he leave when he does the exam."

Tauri nodded. Eli helped her sit up and remove Jonah's jacket. Rachel proceeded to take her vital signs. Then Eli helped Tauri to the scale to be weighed and her height measured.

"Alright, Miss. Hill, just undress from the waist up and put this on," she instructed, handing her a paper gown. "The openings in the back. Rest for a moment and I'll let the doctor know you're ready."

"Thank you, Rachel," they both said in unison.

When the door closed behind the nurse, Eli asked, "are you sure you want me to stay?"

"Yes—for now."

Eli turned his back. He felt more than a little uncomfortable however, but he could understand. She was probably nervous about seeing a doctor who was not her own—and in a completely unfamiliar setting. She looked so helpless, so weak. He wanted to help her get the sweatshirt off but that would be pushing it.

Tauri used all of the energy she had to remove Jonah's large sweatshirt, her t-shirt and bra. She did not know what to think. She almost did not *want* to think. This man, Eli, was taking care of her and moreover she wanted him too. Oscar Brown, her boyfriend of almost three years, ended their relationship when Tauri received the diagnosis of stage two breast cancer. He'd said he couldn't handle the "cancer thing".

Tauri hadn't understood his reaction, because *she* was the one with cancer—not him. Jonah, their aunt, uncle, and the ladies from the Senior Center took turns looking in on her during her treatment. Her longtime friend, Miss Mamie, had told her some men could not stand the pain thinking they might lose someone they care about and so they leave. As far as she was concerned that was just selfish.

Thankfully, the temperature in the room was not too cool. Tauri only shivered a little as she wrapped herself in the paper gown. *Why is he being so nice to me?* She thought that was a good question, so she asked him.

"I'm done," she announced; and when he faced her, she asked, "Eli, why are you so nice to me? Don't you have anyone to take care of or boss around?"

Eli stared then seemed to be searching for an answer. But before he could answer, a knock sounded at the door and then it opened. In walked a very tall, thin, African American man with nut-brown skin, wearing a white lab coat, with reading glasses perched on his wide nose. When he smiled at her, his dark eyes were soft and compassionate. Then he turned to Eli.

"Hi, Eli."

"Leo."

Eli stood and they clapped hands and shared a quick hug. Tauri noticed Eli stood a few inches taller.

"Tauri, this is my good friend, Dr. Leonard Lewis. Leo, this is Tauri Hill—Jonah's sister."

Dr. Lewis gave her a big charming white toothy smile,

"Hello, young lady, nice to meet you. I see the resemblance."

"It's nice to meet you too, Dr. Lewis," Tauri said softly.

The doctor looked at the papers, which were now in a folder.

"Tell me how you're feeling?"

She went on to tell him her symptoms and when she was finished, he wrote something in the folder.

"Alright now I need to listen to your chest."

Then he turned to Eli.

"Eli, could you excuse us for a minute?"

Eli gave Tauri a look and then took her hand.

"I trust him," he said with a smile. "I'll be right outside." She nodded. He opened the door and step out.

Eli paced outside the door for a full twenty minutes before Leo stepped outside. Eli stopped and watched Leo look at him speculatively.

"What?"

"Who is this young lady to you, Eli?"

Leo and Eli had been friends for many years. Eli and Jonah had done an expansive advertising campaign for Leo when he first opened his practice. It worked so well he had to ask an old friend from medical school to share his offices to keep up with the patient load. He and Eli seemed to click from their first meeting. Maybe it was because he and Eli had only four years between them and their values ran along the same lines. They both valued relationships.

Leo stared at Eli as Eli frowned back at him. Eli had not been serious about anyone since Phyllis. He remembered meeting the self-centered, self-absorbed Phyllis a few years back at a fundraiser. Even then, Eli was a young, up and coming advertising executive with a few successful campaigns and all she saw were dollar signs. He'd been blinded by her beauty and forced attentiveness. Thankfully, when Eli started talking about leaving the successful firm to start his own, her true colors came out. She had dropped him like a bad habit.

"I told you," Eli finally answered.

"Yes, I know, she's Jonah's sister. But *who* is she to *you*, brother?"

"What are you talking about, Leo? Jonah had to go out of town unexpectedly on business and asked me to look in on her. I've only known her for two days."

Leo raised his dark thick eyebrows.

"I've known you a while Eli and I can't see you going this distance for a person you've only known for two days."

"I'm just doing what Jonah would have done had he been here."

"Hum," was all Leo said in manner he was unconvinced.

"I'm keeping my promise to look in on her that's all."

"Look, I couldn't let her suffer like that. I had to do something."

When Leo remained silent, Eli finally caught his meaning. His brow rose.

"For goodness sake, Leo!"

His voice was beginning to rise. He realized it and said in a low whisper, "I don't have any feelings for her other than she needs help. I am not in love with her if that's what you think. I only just met her yesterday."

"So what?" Leo said in an equally quiet voice. "Me and Janice knew we wanted each other forever by the end of the first day we met."

Eli knew the story well. He had gotten it firsthand from Mrs. Janice Lewis herself when he had been invited to their home for the first time for a holiday party. The two had shared loving looks all evening and when they were within each other's reach, they were always touching.

Eli was not sure he believed in forever or love at first sight, but he could not deny theirs. His relationships had been few although he had experienced enough of them to know two people had to be very committed to each other to pull off a strong, forever lasting relationship. He was not sure he envisioned nor desired a relationship like theirs. He had not witnessed an especially loving relationship between his parents. In fact, most of the time they seemed to be contentious in nature.

Leo and Janice's obvious affection was completely foreign to him. It was the first time he had witnessed evident love and mutual admiration between a husband and wife.

Eli looked at his good friend and stated emphatically, " she is a sister of a good friend. He asked me to look in on her and that is all I'm doing."

Leo held his hands up in surrender.

"Okay. Okay. I just call it as I see it. I'll let it go," Leo sighed.

"Now, she is going to need someone with her for at least forty-eight hours. She has the beginning symptoms of the flu since she already has the chills and a fever. Next, there will be more sweating then chills."

"I get the picture," Eli said, as he continued to listen.

"For the next twenty-four hours, it's going to be rough."

"But she said she had the flu shot."

"I know. Some people still get sick, especially when their immune system is low or compromised. From what she told me she has been burning the candle at both ends. I gave her a couple of prescriptions. I'll have Hope call them into the local pharmacy—it's in the shopping center near Jonah's place. You know it?" Leo asked and waited as Eli to nodded. "You can pick them up on your way home."

"Thanks, Leo. Is she ready to go?"

Leo looked at the door.

"She should be. Just knock before you go in."

"Thanks again, man, for getting us in on such short notice."

They shook hands and Leo slapped Eli on the back.

"No problem—had a cancellation. Let me know if her fever doesn't break in twenty-four hours."

"Will do."

"Are we watching the big game at your place?"

Without thinking, Eli answered, "No. Jonah's."

"Is he still going for the underdog?"

"You know it."

Leo chuckled.

"See you then—gotta go—pretty busy."

"Alright, man."

Eli watched Leo as he walked down the hall to another door and grabbed a chart from its holder.

Eli tapped on the door.

"Come in," came Tauri's soft and muffled voice.

He opened the door to find her sitting up on the examination table. Her clothes and Jonah's jacket and knit cap were all in place. Her purse in her lap. Eli was surprised at how much more tired she looked.

He smiled and asked, "You ready?"

Tauri slowly nodded. She held out the prescription slip.

"I know," Eli said. "We'll pick them up at the local pharmacy on the way back."

He walked over to her and picked her up. She leaned her head on his shoulder but said nothing as he walked out of the doctor's office heading for his car.

He stopped at the pharmacy, picked up her prescription and drove the short distance to Jonah's condo. Eli took her inside and directly to her room. He removed his overcoat and laid it across a chair near the bed.

"Okay, sweetheart. Put on your nightgown or pajamas," Eli told her.

Tauri looked at him with those big brown eyes of hers. With the weariness and tiredness evident on her face, she shook her head and pointed to the dresser across the room. Eli hesitated. Did she want him to help her change? *'Pull yourself together,'* Eli thought. *'She's sick. You can do this.'*

He wiped his sweaty palms on his slacks. Eli promised himself, when she got better, they would discuss her lack of inhibitions with total strangers. *Just think of this as if she were my patient and I was her nurse.*

Satisfied with the pep talk he'd given himself, Eli turned and walked over to the dresser and pulled open the drawer. It was filled with an assortment of satiny, silky, lacy things. He did not want to touch them but knew he had to filter through them to find something suitable for a sick person, and so far, none of these fit the bill. He had to choose something that would not make him want to take it off her later.

Now he was confused. His pulse raced when his hands touched the silky apparel knowing that it had touched her skin. He heard Tauri say something. He whipped his head around. Tauri was lying down, looking at him.

"The other drawer."

"Oh," is all he could manage. He closed the lace filled drawer and opened the second one down. Three nicely folded stacks of what looked like pajamas, each with a different floral pattern, filled the drawer.

He pulled out the ones with the purple background and scattered yellow sunflowers. He smiled. When he turned around, Tauri had closed her eyes, her legs hung over the side of the bed. He had to move quickly to get her into those pajamas, get food in her stomach, and give her the medicine Leo had prescribed.

Eli placed the pjs on the bed and knelt at Tauri's feet. He removed her shoes leaving her socks in place.

"Tauri, honey."

She opened her eyes.

"We have to get you changed and then you can sleep."

She nodded and said "okay?"

"Okay. Come on, sit up."

When she did, he removed the knit cap. Her dark brown hair was a mass of tangles and curls.

"Let's get you tucked in nice and snug."

He pulled her sweatshirt over her head and was grateful to see a soft light blue t-shirt underneath.

"Can you do the rest?" he asked.

She crossed her arms in front of her and grabbed the bottom of the t-shirt. Her movements were slow and seemed to take every bit of strength she had left but she managed to get the t-shirt over her head. Exhausted, she let her head fall on Eli's shoulder. He closed his eyes at the sight of her lacy black bra which held her full breasts. *I can't unsee* that. He was glad her head was on his shoulder because it was difficult for him to remember what he was supposed to be doing.

Eli let out a deep breath.

"Tauri, you're almost there. Come on, sweetie."

Tauri moaned and put her right arm behind her back in an attempt to undo the clasp of her bra but failed. Eli took a deep breath, then removed her hand and undid the clasp. His hands trembled as he eased the strap down one shoulder then the other. *Oh man!!* He removed the lacy bra from her arms, careful not to disturb her head on his shoulder.

Quickly, he took the pajama top and put it over her head, thankful it did not have buttons. When he had eased her arms in, he laid her down and removed her sweat suit bottom, replacing them with the flowery pajama bottom. *She's just my patient.* He placed her legs in the bed, pulling the covers over her.

"Tauri, I'll be right back. You need to eat and take your medicine. Okay?"

"Okay."

As Eli turned to walk away, Tauri grabbed his arm. He stopped and looked down at her.

"Thank you," she whispered.

He smiled and said, "my pleasure," meaning every word. "I'll be right back."

As Eli warmed the leftover soup, he placed a call to Jonah.

Jonah answered the call after the second ring, "Hey Eli, we're making great progress on the project, but I still won't be able to get back until the weekend."

"Ok, just so you know; I took Tauri to see Leo and he said she most likely has the flu."

"I figured as much."

"Don't worry, bro. I got her."

A little while later, Eli returned to the room with a tray filled with juice, soup and medicine. He urged Tauri to sit up and eat, then he gave her the medicine from the pharmacy.

"Okay, now get some sleep. I need to check in at work and run some errands, but I'll be back."

He pulled a business card from his shirt pocket.

"This is how you can reach me if you need anything. I'm going to put my card right here by the phone."

Tauri nodded; already falling asleep.

"Thank you," said in barely a whisper.

Eli leaned over and kissed her on the forehead and smoothed her tangled hair. He stood up and stared down at her. A feeling of protectiveness and possessiveness was building inside of him.

This was not an unfamiliar feeling to him, for it was the way he felt about his sister and mother. However, this was somehow different. What had he gotten himself into? *'Trouble'* was the word that popped into his head.

Chapter 6

"Good afternoon, Iris. What's on the hot sheet today," Eli asked when he walked in the lobby door.

As usual, in her very efficient way, Iris read off a string of appointments she'd rescheduled and calls that needed to be returned. As she read, Eli turned and walked slowly toward his office. Iris promptly grabbed her handy note pad and pen, and followed him into his office. For the next half-hour, they discussed the projects and the schedule for the rest of the week.

"Iris, I need to work around some of these appointments. I have to take care of a sick friend," Eli announced.

Iris smiled and said, "A female friend, I hope."

Eli returned the smile and said, "Yes, a female friend."

Iris said, "it's about time."

Eli held up his hands.

"It's not like that. Jonah's sister is in town and she became ill. Since Jonah's away, I agreed to...sort of...look in on her."

"Tauri's still here?" Iris asked.

"Oh, you've met her?" Eli asked, trying not to sound anxious.

"What do you know about her?"

"We've talked several times over the phone and then briefly when she arrived. She always calls the office, for Jonah, when he does not answer his cell phone, which is often. As you may know, Tauri's a very accomplished young woman. She works as much and as hard as you and Jonah. She owns two very successful day care centers in California and does a lot of charity work."

"We've talked several times over the phone and then briefly when she arrived. She always calls the office, for Jonah, when he does not answer his cell phone, which is often. As you may know, Tauri's a very accomplished young woman. She works as much and as hard as you and Jonah. She owns two very successful day care centers in California and does a lot of charity work."

"Wow," Eli said, thinking there is a lot about Tauri he did not know.

"Jonah told me she was only here until the Sunday after Thanksgiving," Iris said. "We wanted to have her over for dinner. Did you say she was ill?"

"Yes. She caught a cold on Friday and now it's turned into the flu."

Iris looked at him thoughtfully.

"Oh my. And you're taking care of her?"

"Yes, I am—well, I'm trying. She's a little stubborn."

"From what Jonah told me, Tauri has had to take care of herself for a long time. It's hard for someone to give up control of themselves to someone else. Especially, if she doesn't know you."

Eli remembered Jonah had told him Tauri became his legal guardian when she was only twenty-one years old. Since she was so independent, Eli wondered if she would push him away when she got better. He was beginning to like taking care of her. It even bothered him being away from her for this long. He looked at his watch. In a little over an hour it would be time for her to awake, eat and take her medicine and he intended to be there to make sure she did.

"She's a good woman, you know." Iris said, breaking into his thoughts.

"What?"

"It wouldn't hurt you to find someone to make you happy, Elijah," Iris said in a motherly tone.

Eli knew she meant well, so he did not get offended when, on occasion, she sounded like his mother.

"I'm okay, Iris," he said, tentatively.

Not too long ago, he had admitted to himself something was missing in his life and he that needed a change.

"That's what you told me after Phyllis Emery walked away," Iris said, using her motherly tone again. "All that hussy wanted was all of your time and money—and gifts."

"Yeah," Eli said and smiled at Iris's description of Phyllis.

"Ancient history, Iris."

Iris knew Eli had wanted to change the subject, and so did she. Phyllis had done a number on Eli. She was a beautiful woman and even charming, in the right circumstances, but make her mad and she was a real witch. Iris was glad Eli had told Phyliss of his preparation to leave 'DHP Advertising' to start his own firm. Phyllis had told him he was a fool to leave such a lucrative company to try to make it on his own. Iris thought Phyllis was the fool for leaving a man like Eli. It had hurt Eli but thank the Lord he had not asked her to marry him or gone after her.

Now, Tauri was another matter. Iris had spoken to her on several occasions. Tauri would call Iris when she was worried about Jonah, or whenever she was looking for a special gift for him. She had even questioned Iris when she wanted to know who Jonah was dating. Iris believed Tauri Hill would be good for Eli.

Eli too wanted to change the subject because Iris always got upset when Phyllis' name came up. If Eli really wanted to be truthful with himself, Phyllis's name still caused a twist of pain deep in his gut and a little kick to his pride. Phyllis thought he had lost his mind by wanting to start his own company. Shortly thereafter, she wished him luck and walked out of his life without looking back.

The day she left, he realized their future visions were different and Phyllis had no faith in him or his dreams. She wanted what she thought was a sure thing—for him to keep his position at DHP. An economic shift had caused the company to lose a few clients however with the new incentives and fresh, different approaches, they had managed to hold their own.

Eli's thoughts shifted back to Tauri. For some reason he wondered what her goals in life were. What were her hearts desires and aspirations?

Bringing his mind back to the moment, he stated, "I took Tauri to the doctor this morning and he prescribed some medication for her flu symptoms. He said we would just have to let this thing run its course. Do you have any other suggestions?"

"There are a number of remedies. But something tells me Tauri is not going to go for whiskey in her tea."

"Probably not," Eli chuckled,

"Try some vitamin C—about 1000 milligrams—and Echinacea."

"Leo gave her a prescription for vitamin C."

"Good. Echinacea usually comes in tea form, however there are capsules and liquid forms in some stores. The echinacea will make her sweat a lot but that's good because it helps get some of the impurities out of her."

Eli nodded and looked at his watch again.

"She's grown on you that fast, huh?" Iris said, with a smile.

"It's not unusual for you to fall for her so soon. Don't fight it, Elijah."

Iris closed her notepad, stood up commenting, "life is too short. Live it, Elijah."

Then she was gone.

Eli thought about his conversation with Iris as he ran a few errands. First, he stopped at his place and picked up a change of clothes. Then quickly by the health food store and picked up some echinacea tea and more ingredients for soup.

Iris was right about Tauri.

She'd been trying to push him away and was right not to trust him—partly because she did not know him. But he was pushing back. She challenged him even when she was weak. He liked a woman with guts and internal strength. She had probably developed those traits the hard way with all the experiences she had while raising Jonah.

Eli also had a feeling Iris was right about something else. Tauri had taken care of herself for so long, she probably didn't know how to let anyone else take care of her. It drew him to her like a bear to honey. He smiled as he looked over at the honey in the bag on the front seat of the car. Maybe he should take Iris' advice and let it happen.

Eli quietly opened the door to Jonah's home and went to work preparing Tauri's dinner and tea. When he was done, he carried the soup and tea into Tauri's room. He could not believe she was still asleep. He had been gone the entire afternoon and it was now eighteen minutes after six.

He put the soup and tea down on the nightstand and looked down at Tauri. She looked so innocent and fragile. Those weren't the right words, but it was all that came to mind. Her hair was a mass of curls and tangles that only enhanced her natural beauty.

He ran the back of his hand on her cheek and forehead. They were both cool—a very good sign. She moved and her hand automatically covered his and held it there as she tried to settle back into her sleep. Something in Eli's chest warmed. He itched to pull her into his arms and promise her he would make her feel better.

Instead he called softly, "Tauri, Tauri."

She squeezed his hand tighter and tighter, then snuggled deeper into the covers.

"Tauri, sweetheart. It's time to eat and take your medicine again. Come on. Wake up."

With little effort, Eli freed his hand and sat on the edge of the bed. He leaned over and kissed her temple.

"Wake up, sleepy head," he said.

That seemed to do the trick. She stirred.

"Come on, Sleeping Beauty. You have to eat and take your medicine. Sit up."

He pushed a couple of pillows behind her back. Tauri sat up.

"There we are."

"Eli, I just want to sleep," she said groggily.

"Later. Now you eat and then you take your medicine."

She yawned and stared sleepily at him.

"If I eat and take my medicine, will you leave me alone and let me sleep?"

He barely held back a smile. She was going to fight until the end.

"Yes."

She scooted back against the pillows. He spoon fed her the soup, just as he had done before.

"Are you cold?"

"A little."

"Here, finish this."

He handed her the almost empty soup bowl.

"I'll be right back."

When he returned, he had a comforter and a glass of orange juice. He sat the juice on the nightstand and gently draped the cover over the bed.

"Did you finish it all?"

"Yes, sir."

He smiled.

"Now your medicine."

When she took it, Eli offered her the tea and sat back down on the bed. She tasted it and scrunched her nose.

"What is this?"

"Tea. It will make you feel better. Drink it."

She took a cautious sip, her face furled up into a wrinkle, "But it's so nasty."

He frowned at her.

"Drink it, Tauri," he demanded.

"Do you order people around this much at work?"

"No, I don't get the chance because they do their jobs."

"So, I get the benefit of all of your pent-up frustration from not having anybody to order around?"

"You know what," Eli said, narrowing his eyes, "For a sick person, you sure do talk a lot. Drink your tea, Tauri."

She rolled her big brown eyes at him.

"I know you didn't just roll your eyes at me, did you, Tauri Hill?"

When she said nothing and just drank the tea, he said, "Good answer."

When the tea was gone and Tauri had drank some orange juice, she pulled back the covers and started to get out of bed.

"And where do you think you're going?"

The frown returned to his brow. This time Tauri reached up and rubbed his forehead until the wrinkles were smooth.

"Eli, I need to go to the bathroom. You made me drink a ton of liquids. I wouldn't be surprised if I'm going to be getting up all night."

"Okay. Here let me help you."

Eli took her arm and held it like a fragile piece of glass.

"I'm not going to break, Eli," she said as she stood.

"I thought your body might be sore. Leo told me that was one of the symptoms of the flu," he said, as they walked to the short distance to the bathroom.

"I am a little sore but not so bad on my arms," she confessed.

He walked her to the toilet and stood, not sure what to do next. Tauri looked at him.

"Eli, I think I can take it from here."

"Oh, okay. I'll be right outside."

"Thanks."

When she was done, he was waiting by the door. He escorted her to the bed and considered tucking her in but thought better of it. He repositioned and fluffed the pillows and smoothed the sheets. Tauri thought before she climbed into bed, '*who is this man?*' Turning to Eli and again said, "thank you, Eli. You're taking such good care of me."

"Even though I'm a little pushy?"

"Yes, but the word is bossy."

Tauri audibly exhaled when she settled into the bed once more. Eli pulled the covers up to her chin. He bent over and kissed her on the temple.

"Get some sleep."

Later, Eli made himself a sandwich and returned some emails while he ate. The return calls would have to wait until tomorrow morning—all except the one from Jonah. He dialed his cell number.

Jonah answered on the third ring; "Jonah Hill."

"Hey man, it's Eli. Did I catch you at a bad time?"

Eli always started his call as such when it took Jonah a while to answer the phone.

"No, Eli. It's been a really long day. Almost nothing went as planned. That's why I called you so late."

"Do you need any help from me or Iris? I could send one of the team over."

"No. It's just that we have too many temperamental actors and actresses on the set. They act as if they are going for an academy award. The director threatened to quit twice today."

Eli chuckled. He knew how some shoots could go. It was amazing how long it took to shoot a thirty-second spot. But he knew as well as Jonah, it only takes a split-second to capture the viewer's attention. Every second of commercial time mattered. The customer must be assured the advertising is going to get their message across to the public resulting in sales.

"So, it sounds like you had a little talk with them."

Jonah could be hard when someone messed with his baby and this project was definitely his baby.

"Yes, I told them all if tomorrow is anything like today, I'm going to fire the entire cast and start over."

"I bet that got their attention."

"Yeah, you can say that, but I'll see tomorrow. How are things there?"

"Iris has the office under control."

"What do you mean? You're not there?"

"No. I took Tauri to see Leo this morning and she has the flu. He said she needed someone to stay with her the next few days."

"Ahh, so that's why she's not answering her cell. Maybe I should come back early?" Jonah said, his voice filled with worry.

"I think I have it under control and besides, I don't think your sister would appreciate that."

"I don't know, Eli," Jonah said. "Tauri can be difficult when she's not feeling well, especially if you try to take care of her."

"A small detail you forgot to mention."

Jonah chuckled.

"Tauri can be a handful. You wouldn't think she could be that bad having the flu."

"Yeah, I want to let you know that I intend to sleep on the sofa tonight just in case she needs anything."

"Eli you don't have to do that. I'm sure Tauri's had the flu before. She can handle it."

Eli could tell Jonah did not mean to sound uncaring about his sister's health. He wasn't not sure about letting a man; even his good friend sleep in his home alone with his sister all night.

"Jonah, I could leave her here alone. I'm sure she could take care of herself if she had to, but I promised you that I would look in on her."

Eli decided to cut to the heart of Jonah's concern.

"And I promise to be a complete gentleman."

"I know Eli, but you understand what I'm saying."

"I got it. Don't worry, Jonah, I am not going to seduce a sick woman. Besides, sick or not Tauri will let me know if I cross the line."

Jonah chuckled again.

"You're right about that. I'll see how the shoot goes tomorrow and maybe I can be back by Friday."

"Sounds good. Keep me posted."

"You too. Goodnight, Eli."

"Night, Jonah."

Eli shook his head as he disconnected the call. He did not know why he felt obligated to tell Jonah he was spending the night at his place with his sister. It just seemed like the right thing to do. He questioned himself a few times about leaving her alone. He knew if he left her there, he would not really get any sleep because he would be up all night wondering if she was alright.

Eli yawned then looked at his watch. It was almost ten thirty and he was beat. He changed into a long sleeve cotton gray t-shirt and a pair of gray sweat pant bottoms.

His long legs stretched out over the coffee table with his laptop opened in his lap. Thirty minutes later, he yawned again, closed his email, turned off his laptop and went to the bathroom to brush his teeth. He went back to the living room and pulled the comforter from Jonah's bed up over him and stretched out on the sofa. His eyes closed.

It seemed a short while later, through the haze of sleep, Eli heard someone call his name. It was soft and sweet, like a caress.

"Eli."

There it was again, this time it sounded like a distress cry for help. Eli came fully awake.

"Tauri?"

He jumped up from the sofa in an instant and was in her room in less in a few seconds. When his eyes adjusted to the dark room, he could see that she was tossing and turning, calling his name. He went to her bedside and turned on the lamp on the nightstand. Tauri's face and hair were drenched in sweat. He tried to remember what Leo and Iris told him. Both had told him she would sweat as her fever broke.

He felt her forehead. It was damp but cool, meaning she no longer had a fever. Eli went to the bathroom, grabbed a clean hand towel and saturated it with cold water. Moving back to the bed he wiped her face and neck. When he pulled back the covers, he could see that her clothes were plastered to her body. She began to shiver.

"Eli, I'm cold."

Her eyes were partially closed as she hugged herself.

"I know, sweetie. I have to get you into some dry clothes."

He placed the covers back over her and walked over to the dresser. He pulled out a long-sleeved flowered gown and went in the bathroom to get a dry towel. He had to get her out of those wet clothes. He pulled back the covers gently and removed her top and wiped the sweat from her body.

He put the gown over her head, pulled it down over her midsection and removed her pajama bottoms. Toweling her dry, he pulled the gown down and pulled the covers up over her. She snuggled into the dry pillows he had also shifted over.

Satisfied, he straightened and clicked the light off, then turned to leave the room.

"Eli?"

It was just a whisper, yet he heard it. He was back at her bedside in a heartbeat. Kneeling, he reached up and turned on the light again.

"Yes, sweetheart, is everything alright?" he asked, smoothing back her damp hair. She grabbed his hand.

"Stay with me."

It was a simple statement but carried so much weight. He swallowed. He looked over at the chair near the dresser.

"Okay, I'll sit right here in this chair."

"No, I need you here," Tauri said, patting the other side of the bed.

"Are you sure, Tauri?"

"Yes," she affirmed and patted the bed again.

Eli blew out a breath and went around to the other side of the bed pulling back the top cover then climbed in. He figured he would be safe with her under the covers if he kept all his clothes on. He reached over and switched the light off again. He settled down into the bed. Tauri tried to get close to him but the layers of covers were preventing it.

Tauri tugged lightly at the covers. Eli sighed, pulled back the rest of the covers, eased back into bed and pulled the covers up over them. Tauri draped her arm over his chest, her leg came up over his legs and she nestled her head into his shoulder. Eli's entire body stiffened. He knew he was not getting any sleep tonight.

The next morning, Eli's internal clock automatically woke him up at six thirty-one. It took him a minute to get his bearings. He blinked then looked around. He was in Tauri's bedroom, in her bed. He looked down at her body curled snuggly against him. He tensed. Now he remembered. Tauri had asked several times until he climbed into bed with her.

He looked down again at Tauri's sleeping face, peaceful, trusting. Automatically, he pulled her closer. It felt good. It felt right.

Suddenly a flash of panic raced through him. *'Jonah's going to kill me. What was I thinking?'* This was Jonah's sister. He was supposed to be taking care of her not taking advantage of her. He did not want any attachments or distractions right now, did he? What did he want? More to the point, did he even know?

His only role models had been his parents who had been together forever but he hadn't seen any great love between them as he grew up. He and his sister watched them for years be polite in front of guests and other relatives. In the privacy of their own home, they argued and disagreed on this and criticized on that.

To him, they seemed to be a very neutral couple. He did not want a complacent relationship but one that grew as their lives grew together.

Tauri stirred, opened her eyes and looked at him. Surprise then confusion registered in her sleepy stare.

"Eli...um...what are you doing in my bed?"

"I couldn't take the whining anymore," he said sarcastically.

She frowned as she pulled back a little but did not move from his embrace.

"Whining? I don't whine."

He smiled down at the frown that formed above her brown eyes. *'She must be getting her strength back.'* He could see something else in those beautiful eyes—irritation.

"Apparently, you do, when you're not feeling well."

Tauri's eyes grew wide and her heart pounded as she looked into his handsome face. *'What a way to wake up.'* She wanted to run her hand across the short stubble on his strong sexy chin. Eli squeezed her.

"You look better now than you did last night. I think you'll live."

"I feel a lot better, thanks."

"Good, I'm going to fix you breakfast before I go to work. You need to take your medicine."

"I don't like taking medicine. I feel fine."

"And you'll continue to stay that way if you take your medicine, Tauri Hill," Eli said, the tone of his voice leaving no room for argument.

She looked at him as if she was not convinced. Her body helped him prove his point when she sneezed into his shirt.

"I'm sorry. Excuse me."

He reached over grabbed a tissue and gave it to her. He continued to hold her as he looked down at her.

"That's okay. Bless you. I cannot believe you are so stubborn. I bet your man doesn't get this much flack."

She looked away.

"I don't have a man."

She tried to pull away, but Eli would not let her.

"I'm sorry, sweetheart, I didn't mean to pry. I was just teasing."

He pulled her closer and kissed her forehead.

"But stop being stubborn. Take your medicine."

He kissed her forehead again, then released her, got up off the bed and walked out of the room.

Tauri was speechless. In less than one week, Eli had all but taken over her life. Whenever he was around her, she lost the strong front she had always worn like a shield. So many people had tried taking advantage of her over the years, assuming because of her youth and raising a teenaged boy, she had not known what she was doing.

Of course, she had help sometimes from the ladies at the senior center and treasured her friends but ultimately the responsibility was hers. Jonah had found their father's estranged sister, Aunt Ellie and her husband, Uncle John, on social media when she had been diagnosed with cancer. In the short time she had come to know Eli, she did not feel or think he would ever take advantage of her.

Slowly, she rose and headed for the shower. She did feel better in contrast to last night which was a little blurry. All she remembered was being very hot and most definitely did not remember whining for him to sleep with her. She grew warm thinking she had missed an opportunity to enjoy it.

Tauri looked at herself in the mirror. Her hair was a horrible mess, but Eli looked at her as if she were the most beautiful and cherished woman in the world.

"What are you doing girl?" Tauri asked herself, aloud. "You don't want a man in your life right now—he'll want all your time."

She assumed he would be jealous, just like Oscar had been.

"You'll get involved and then he'll leave you."

She let out a deep breath. It just would not work.

Eli heard Tauri's shower running. He decided to finish breakfast, take a quick shower then head out for work.

Later, as he emerged from Jonah's room ready to begin the day, Eli saw Tauri sitting at the table eating. She wore a pair of purple sweatpants, a matching top and purple socks. He released the breath he was holding. She had combed her hair and pulled it back in a ponytail. She was definitely the most beautiful woman he'd seen in a long time.

"I see your appetite is back."

Tauri turned, startled. Her mouth was filled with grits and eggs. He chuckled.

"I'm sorry. Please don't choke. I'll have to explain to Leo and Jonah what happened."

She swallowed, then took a sip of her juice.

"Thank you for the breakfast."

He walked over and stood in front of her. He put his hand on her temple and her cheek, frowning. She reached up and smoothed the frown away.

"What's the prognosis, doctor?"

He grabbed her hand and pulled her up from the chair.

"You are progressing nicely."

Then he kissed her. Not on the temple like before but very lightly on the lips.

She pulled back in protest, "Eli, I don't want to get you sick."

"I think you're past the contagious stage."

He bent his head to kiss her again. This time she leaned into him. Her mouth opened and he deepened the kiss.

In her mind, she wanted to tell him anything between them would not work, but instead she heard herself moan.

Eli pulled away and looked down at Tauri, her eyes were closed. She opened them then frowned. He smiled down at her and smoothed the lines out with his forefinger—just as she had done with him earlier.

"What's the matter, Tauri?"

"Why did you stop?"

Her voice was soft but laced with irritation.

"Because I don't think either of us is ready for where this might lead."

Eli held back a smile. One hand came up to cup her face, the other held tightly around her waist. Even though he wanted to stop the kiss from going too far, Eli still liked the feel of her body against his.

Tauri put her head against his neck and exhaled. She thought about what he said, and thought, *'he's right.'* They had just met each other and subconsciously she already wanted to get him in bed. Tauri closed her eyes to the knowledge of a long-hidden part of her had been awakened. She remembered Oscar commenting she had not responded to him the way he needed or wanted her to. What was she missing with him?

In her remembrance, it became apparent what she had missed was sense of trust and ultimately love. When she was with Eli, she couldn't *stop* responding. Eli was stroking her back and she was mesmerized. He looked so handsome in his navy-blue suit and light blue shirt. The mosaic design in his tie with light blue and navy pulled the two together.

"Eli?"

"Humm?"

"If you don't want this to go any further between us, you should stop stroking my back."

"In a minute," he quietly murmured as he continued to stroke as his cheek lay against her hair.

"Eli!"

"Okay, but I need another one of these first."

He kissed her with such softness and care. To Tauri's way of thinking—well, frankly, she could *not* think. Tauri pushed against his chest. She had to get her distance. Eli was pulling her in fast. She pushed again, this time he let her go. She stepped back, breathing fast.

They stared at each other for a while. Tauri wanted to take away some of the tension between them so she asked, "Eli, what happened to my pajamas?"

She saw him stiffen. His eyes looked away, then back. Knowing full well he'd helped her into them in the first place. He cleared his throat.

"You called out to me in your sleep...and you were drenched in sweat, and your pjs were soaked. I had to take...remove those wet clothes because..."

Her looked up at him, and she tried to hold back a smile.

"Because?"

He looked so apologetic.

"Because you were shivering, and I didn't want you to get worse."

She gave him a radiant smile, and asked, "did you look?"

"No. Yes. I mean I tried not to look."

He tried to loosen his tie. She cupped his cheek then kissed it.

"Thank you, Eli."

Eli relaxed. A silence lay between them once again. Tauri knew it would be a mistake to think she could become involved in a relationship with him and he find out later that she could not give it the attention he thought it should have.

He lived here and she would be in California within the next couple of days. It would never work so she had to stop it now.

"You were right, Eli. I don't have room in my life right now for a relationship."

He looked at her for a few seconds. They had not had a chance to talk about a relationship since they had only known each other for less than a week. At least that is what his head kept telling him. But his heart was saying something completely different. It felt so good being around her. Who would not want to be in this woman's life? She was beautiful, talented, intelligent, independent, and sharp. Although, she was not feeling well, Tauri was a ray of sunshine in his life.

What would it be like if she were one hundred percent again? It was something to look forward to, but he did not want to get into a relationship with challenges from the very start. She had her businesses and he was preparing to launch his own firm.

Eli's brow wrinkled, and he finally answered, "neither do I," before clearing his throat and looking away. "I'd better get going. I have a meeting this morning."

"Okay, of course," she agreed. "Did you eat?"

"I'll pick up something on the way. Make sure you eat all of your breakfast."

He grabbed his laptop, keys, phone and as he headed for the door he turned.

"Tauri, did you take your medicine?"

Tauri smiled, and answered, "yes, Eli, I took my medicine."

He smiled back.

"Good girl. I'll check back later this afternoon."

She wanted to tell him that would not be necessary, but she said, "Thanks. Have a good day."

"Thanks," Eli said and then he was gone.

Chapter 7

Eli was aware of the excitement buzzing around the conference room, although it had not affected him. Their new client wanted to get started earlier than planned, so Eli had to momentarily pull Jonah from the New York client, in order to do an impromptu video conference.

Jonah asked Eli for an extra hour to put together a presentation, and what a presentation it was. Jonah had also requested the New York crew take a two-hour lunch in order to prepare the presentation. He spent an hour with the team in Chicago tossing ideas back and forth before presenting their ideas to the client. The client was so pleased with the presentation, they wanted to begin right away.

As the team discussed making their ideas a reality, Eli's thoughts kept drifting back to Tauri and the conversation they'd had that morning. She did not have room in her life right now for a relationship. Which meant she did not have room in her life for...him. He had done it again—he'd offered his heart and had it crushed. What made him think, after less than one week, he would find the woman who would touch his soul like no other woman ever had?

Eli should not have been surprised. After all, he *had* set Tauri up, although her response was not what he expected. He knew she was as equally affected by the kiss they shared but she had pulled back. She was running from him, but why? He had not pushed her that hard and truly believed he had behaved as a perfect gentleman. He hadn't tried to take advantage of her, even though there had been several opportunities.

The team was busy brain-storming in the conference room and in the midst of all the busy work, Eli's thoughts hung on Tauri and he decided someone must have hurt her. Her tendency to push him away was an effort to try and make sure that it wouldn't happen again. Tauri would be leaving to go back to her life in California as soon as she felt better, and *he* had to let her go, didn't he? He had no claim on her and as she said, she did not have time for a relationship. He was not the type of man who stood in anyone's way—or was he? Perhaps there was more to this than he was willing to admit.

Eli did know this about himself; he was determined and always went after what he wanted. Most of the time, he got it. Why should this time be any different? He realized he definitely wanted Tauri Hill and he was going to get her.

"Mr. Thornton?"

Eli looked up into Iris' inquisitive stare.

"Yes?"

"When would you like to hold the first meeting?"

Eli looked around the table. Nine pair of expectant eyes stared at him.

"Mr. Hill will be back in town by the end of the week. I would like a few days for him to get a creative team together to create a directional plan for the campaign. We can meet next week to hash out the specific details. As usual, we will then run it by DH before presenting it to the client."

Iris, ever efficient said, "what about next Wednesday at two thirty PM?"

Eli knew Iris had his and Jonah's schedule, so he confirmed the appointment.

"That will be fine. Any objections?"

He looked around the table as everyone checked their electronic devices and schedules. The answers from all present were affirmative. Eli stood, signaling the meeting was adjourned. Hands were shaken, appreciation extended, and the team returned to their respective offices.

Eli and Iris remained at the table.

"How's Tauri doing," Iris asked.

Eli looked up from the papers in front of him.

"She's doing a lot better. That tea seemed to do the trick."

He busied himself by gathering his notes.

"Yes, it always worked well for my family."

Eli could feel Iris watching him.

"Eli, what's bothering you?"

He looked up thinking he could lie but decided against it.

"Is it that obvious?"

Iris was sharp but he wondered if everyone else noticed also.

"A little. Want to talk about it?" Iris asked

"It's Tauri."

"You said she was getting better."

"Oh, she is. It's just that…"

"She got to you," Iris said.

Eli stopped shuffling the papers and walked over to a window that took up one of the walls in the conference room. He shoved one of his hands in his pocket.

"Eli, you look like a man in denial. You think it's too soon, don't you?"

He turned to face her.

"I don't know what to think, Iris. She says she doesn't have room in her life for a relationship but the signals I'm getting from her say something completely different."

"She's probably a little scared," Iris said. "I remember Jonah telling me about a relationship she was in a few years back that had not worked out well and ended badly. Maybe she is just being cautious."

Eli turned back to look out the window. A spark of hope ran through him and he sighed, "you're probably right. I understand wanting to be cautious and independent."

He understood it well. Independence was one of his primary motives in wanting his own firm so badly he could almost taste it. Being dependent on someone else, to give their approval on something you knew would exceed the client's expectations, only to then have the firm take most of the profit and all the credit, wasn't what Eli wanted for himself.

"If you really want something to happen between the two of you, give her time to get used to it," Iris said as she stood, and turned to leave then stopped. "Your calendar is pretty full today, but I can move a few things around if you want to leave early."

He looked at Iris and smiled.

"Thanks, I don't want to be out too much while Jonah's gone."

"No problem. Pick up some fresh flowers on your way home tonight. They always brighten my day."

Eli laughed.

"You never stop do you?"

"What can I say," Iris said returning the smile. "I'm a hopeless romantic."

As Tauri waited expectantly for Eli, she thought back, fondly, remembering her parent's relationship. Theirs had been one of love, devotion, and dedication. Felicia Smith's family moved into her childhood neighborhood after her father secured a job at a local factory. Felicia met Dwayne Hill in middle school and from that day on they had been inseparable.

Tauri smiled as she could hear her dad saying Felicia was the sugar in his coffee. In her mind's eye, she wanted the same type of relationship—one built on appreciation and love. She was sure she never had that kind of relationship with Oscar.

As she and Jonah were growing up, they would always go to their parents with a problem or when they had gotten into trouble. Their parents would discuss the challenge and jointly come to a solution before making a decision.

Tauri and Jonah trusted their wise advice and honored the loving undercurrent in their family. Tauri's parents modeled what a healthy marriage looked like, even in the ups and downs of life. She was determined to have the same kind of marriage and knew it would be a work in process.

When her father suddenly died of a heart attack, the entire family had been devastated. The following year her mother died, further deepening the family's loss. The Coroner's Report listed her death as heart failure, however Tauri strongly believed her mom had died of loneliness and a broken heart. She knew, loving someone so deeply was rare but not impossible. Looking back, she also realized she had no deep love for Oscar and was not sure if it was really love at all.

While she was guarded with Eli, she felt a renewed hope of feeling the wholeness of future love. Eli had shown her such tenderness. Could it be, the wall around her heart was slowly cracking? This was a momentary, fleeting thought as the reality of the distance between them and her priorities became more focused. She really didn't want a relationship right now.

Tauri looked out of Jonah's living room window at the gloomy afternoon weather. It matched the mood she had been in all day. She closed her eyes and thought of what she had said to Eli this morning before he left for work. Tauri had taken a nap after she had finished the breakfast Eli prepared for her.

She had awakened with a start when Eli called her mid-day to check on her. She had wanted to explain her comments from their earlier morning conversation but thought better of it. She was sure she had hurt him and assumed he wanted something more between them. The way he made sure she had eaten her lunch and taken her medicine warmed her heart.

She opened her eyes after a quick nap and looked at the clock. It was almost six thirty. He said he would come by and check on her after work. She wiped her hands on her jeans. How would he react tonight when he came by? Would he be detached and courteous or would he not come at all?

As she prepared dinner, she prayed Eli had not changed his mind about coming over. *'I should apologize to him,'* she thought.

Eli's tender and diligent care of her felt so good and comforting. *'Why was she running?'* She'd had people around to care for her when she had gone through cancer recovery and treatment, but it was not the same.

She could only compare Eli's actions to Oscar who always expected *her* to take care of *him*. She had not minded since she had been responsible and cared for Jonah since he was fifteen. It was a natural shift for her when Jonah went away to college to refocus on caring for Oscar.

'Men were all the same; aren't they?' Tauri asked herself? Didn't they want your undivided attention when you were with them? If Eli saw how busy her life was, he would do the same thing Oscar had done. *'He'll leave; won't he?'* He would complain about not being important enough for her to spend any quality time with him. *'But maybe he'll be different.'*

There were just too many doubts to allow her to think about having a long-distance relationship. She was dedicated to her work and refused to give up this dedication along with the things she loved doing for others.

She jumped at the sound of the doorbell. Eli had a key— why would he ring the bell? On the way to the door, Tauri checked her hair in the mirror next to the door. Her nose was still sore and her eyes a little red but, overall, she looked okay. She glanced down at her blue jeans and orange sweater. Satisfied with her reflection, she opened the door.

Eli did not know what he expected but the beautiful woman now smiling up at him was not it. The words she had said this morning had floated around in his head all day.

They stared at each other for a moment before Eli said, "Good evening."

"Good evening, Eli."

Tauri looked down at the beautiful vase filled with a variety of wildflowers.

"Are those for me?"

He chuckled, deciding not to take all the credit.

"Iris suggested them. I see you feel better."

"Much, thanks to you."

"No. You give me too much credit. You look nice."

"Thank you, please come in."

Tauri stepped back so he could enter.

"Please let me take those."

He handed her the bouquet, removed his overcoat, and hung it in the small closet near the living room. He turned and closely watched her as she walked away. The sweater and jeans she wore hugged every contour of her lush body. Her hair was pulled back and secured at the base of her neck with a bright orange barrette. *Wouldn't I like to come home to that picture every day?* He pushed the thought away as quickly as it appeared.

"Something smells good."

She turned and smiled at him as she sat the vase on the counter.

"I thought I'd cook dinner for you since you've taken such good care of me."

Touched, Eli took two steps then placed his hand ever so lightly on the side of her face.

"You didn't have to do that," he said. "You need your rest."

Her breathing stopped, she closed her eyes as a small shiver ran through her body.

Alarmed, Eli put his other hand on her other cheek. "Tauri, are you alright?"

When she did not answer him, Eli said, "Tauri answer me. You are not well enough to cook. I knew you were moving too fast. You have not completely recovered ..."

Tauri opened her eyes, then released a sighed. She regarded the serious expression on Eli's face. She reached up and smoothed the lines on his brow and smiled.

"Eli, I feel fine. My nose is a little runny, but I haven't been coughing as much. I took a nap today and had frequent breaks while I cooked."

Eli relaxed but the frown returned.

"You still didn't need to cook me dinner."

"I really wanted to show you my appreciation for all you've done for me...and for Jonah," Tauri said.

Eli pulled her close and kissed her on the forehead. He smiled as his hands moved up and down her arms.

" You are only the first *person* I've taken care of. When I was a kid, I used to be the neighborhood vet. I think I was about ten, when my dog, Buddy, got hit by a car. They left him on the side of the road with a broken leg. My parents didn't have the money to take him to the vet, so I splinted his leg and spoon fed him until he was well again."

Tauri was even more amazed by this man who, in one short week, had turned her simple world upside down.

"So, the neighborhood kids brought their sick pets to Dr. Eli?" she joked.

Eli laughed and said, "yes, and my mother would have a fit every time I told her I needed to have the animal stay overnight to keep an eye on them to make sure they were alright."

"What did your dad say?"

Eli moved his hands to her waist, his fingers touched in the middle of her back. They were standing there talking as if they did this every evening after a long workday.

It felt so right to him. He felt comfortable telling her about his childhood—something he had never felt with any other woman. None of them had ever seemed interested but for some reason he knew Tauri would want to hear.

Somehow, he wanted her to know more about his life. What would it be like to do this every day for the rest of his life?
To hide his thoughts, Eli looked over her head into space as if he were searching for the memory.

"My dad was always on my side and then he would tell my mom," he deepened his voice as he imitated his dad, 'Let the boy be, Lizzy! You never know, he might be a veterinarian one day.'"

"Why aren't you a veterinarian? Tauri asked. "It sounds as if you love animals a lot."

He looked down at her.

"I do love animals, but I wanted to travel and meet people. Although, I don't travel as much as I used to when I started working in advertising, I do enough."

"You said your dad was always on your side then. What about now?"

Eli's lips became firm and a frown lined his brow.

"My dad and I are good, and he really supports me. My mom supports me too only in a different way. She thinks it's time for me to get married and start a family. While dad agrees, he also understands my business vision."

"Oh," Tauri said, then averted her eyes and stepped back out of his embrace.

As they stared at each other, her words from that morning came back to haunt her. *"You were right, Eli. I don't have room in my life right now for a relationship."*

Tauri cleared her throat, and told Eli, "we should eat before the food gets cold."

She turned and walked into the kitchen.

Eli decided he most definitely wanted Tauri Hill in his life. He would have to find out why she was running away from him. She had let him touch her too easily to not to want it. Whatever it was, he would find out.

Tauri had prepared a light dinner with what she found in Jonah's refrigerator and cabinets. When she had first arrived, she had only bought enough groceries for Thanksgiving dinner. Jonah did not cook much although she had taught him how. Most of the time he ate out, but she found some frozen chicken and broccoli in the freezer. There were potatoes and some yams left over from Thanksgiving. A few spices and a can of cream of chicken soup and she had herself a dinner. She hoped Eli liked it.

As they ate, Tauri kept looking at Eli for a reaction to the meal.

"This is delicious Tauri, thank you."

Tauri exhaled. She hadn't realized how important the meal was to her until now.

"You're welcome. I'm glad you like it."

Eli thought the expression in her eyes were part relief and part joy. There was almost a glow about her. He noticed a little weariness around her eyes but that was to be expected. She had probably used all her strength to cook dinner for him.

When they finished with their meal, Eli helped Tauri clean the kitchen. He had to insist she sit down and let him finish. He smiled as he looked over at her sitting on the stool. She was actually pouting.

When they finished, Eli decided it would be best to leave because he wanted to kiss more than just her forehead. Besides, after their morning conversation, he thought it best to try to remain neutral even though his heart was telling him something else.

Eli dried his hands and folded the dish towel. Tauri still sat on the stool at the bar watching him.

"I should be going," Eli finally told her. It's been a long day and...

"Eli, would you like to watch a movie with me?" Tauri asked.

Tauri watched as Eli picked up his suit jacket from the back of his dinner chair.

"Do you think that is a good idea?"

She knew what he meant but she said, "I don't see the harm in two people watching a movie together."

She did not want him to leave just yet. When he gave her an incredulous look, Tauri said, "we're just going to watch a movie. There shouldn't be any harm in that."

Eli stood in silence. Tauri walked over and took his hand.

"Come on. You can relax for a little while before you go."

"That won't be easy."

"I promise I won't do anything to make you feel uncomfortable."

Just being in the same room with Tauri made Eli uncomfortable. The thought she may not want him in her life made him even more uncomfortable.

As they walked to the sofa, Tauri held his hand and kept her eyes on his. She took a deep breath.

"Eli, I'm sorry for what I said this morning."

He shook his head, saying, "you don't need..."

She squeezed his hand with both of hers. "My life back home is very busy. It would not be fair to have a man get my leftovers. When I take anything on, I give it one hundred and ten percent. You're too nice not to have a woman who can't give you her complete attention."

Eli tossed his jacket onto a nearby chair and pulled Tauri into his arms. His lips were on hers before his brain knew what was happening. She was so concerned with his wellbeing she was willing to be alone rather than to hurt him later. He thought that her brother would *want* to be selfish. *'She's not being selfish. She's being kind.'*

He heard himself moan as her body relaxed and she melted into him. He drew his arms tighter around her and pulled her closer.

Eli willed her to open to him. As if on cue, she opened her mouth to allow him to deepen the kiss.

She drank him in with such ease it scared her. He was so gentle. He was such a giving man, never asking anything for himself, always respecting her in every way. Tauri hated to break the connection but she had to breathe.

When she pushed back, he loosened his hold on her but only a little.

"Eli," she said, her breathing labored. "We'd better stop."

Eli tried to get control of his breathing. He closed his eyes and nodded his head then leaned it against hers. He felt that each time he kissed Tauri his control was weakening. He wanted to be near her. He would not push but he wanted to. He had never *pushed* any of the women he had been with. Eli also had to admit he had never felt this way about any other woman he had ever been with either.

He held his head up.

"Tauri?"

When she looked up at him, he said, "I need to go."

Disappointment shown clearly in her eyes and she apologized.

"Please, I'm sorry I let you kiss me. I promise it won't happen again."

He smiled. He bent to kiss her forehead then paused, before asking, "may I?"

"Yes," she prompted, "but only if you'll stay."

"You don't play fair," he groaned.

"Maybe not, but that's the condition."

They stared at each other for a while longer before Eli said

"Okay. I'll stay. What movie are we watching?"

Her smile was dazzling

"'*It's A Wonderful Life*' of course."

"Of course."

He kissed her on the forehead again then released her. He blew out a sigh. *'This is going to be a long evening.'*

George Bailey had just jumped into the icy cold water to save Clarence, his guardian angel, when Tauri tried to fight back a yawn. Then Eli followed suit. He removed his shoes and reclined back on the sofa, stretching his long legs out in front of him. Tauri was curled up on the opposite end of the sofa. Eli paused the movie when she stood and excused herself then went to her bedroom.

When she returned Eli saw she had retrieved a comforter from her bed. He looked up and said, "we can look at this another time if you're tired."

"No, Eli," she said hugging the comforter to her chest. "I...I leave for home tomorrow afternoon."

Eli reached up, took her hand, and pulled her down on top of his prone body. She was so surprised she let go of the comforter.

Tauri was alarmed at first by the stern expression on his face. She thought he would be mad but what she saw instead was hurt and her heart cried. However, it would be much more hurtful later when he saw how busy her life was and demanded time that she could not give him.

She closed her eyes to block out his penetrating stare as he held her to his chest.

"Tauri," he said softly.

When she did not look at him, he softly said, "look at me sweetheart."

When she did, he tightened his hold on her.

"Why did you wait until now to tell me you're leaving tomorrow? Why so soon? You're feeling *that* well?"

"I feel fine. I didn't know how to...I thought it would be best before...," she said and paused.

Eli finished her statement.

"Before things got out of hand?"

"Eli, I like you but that's not always enough," Tauri told him. "A relationship is a lot of work and right now, I am so busy and so are you. Besides, a long-distance relationship—how long would that last? I don't want us to end up hurting each other."

Eli continued to look at her thinking about what she had said. She was leaving when he had just gotten used to taking care of her. Before Tauri, his life had been all about his family and work. He only thought seriously about his single life when his mother would bring up the subject of grandkids. He did not dare think of Tauri as the mother of his children or that she would be his forever after life partner.

He pulled her closer. She was running from him and he would have to let it go for now. Tonight, they would enjoy each other's company and think about the future later. He drew her head down onto his chest and pulled the comforter over their bodies.

Eli took long even breaths to calm his fears of never being able to see her again. He would not think about it now. He would just enjoy the feel of her on top of his body. He bent his head and kissed Tauri on the forehead and buried his face in her hair. He inhaled her scent so he would remember.

Eli's eyes drifted over to the television screen and watched as George Bailey began to understand what Bedford Falls would have been like had he never existed. He tightened his hold just a little around Tauri as she fell asleep in his arms. She looked so peaceful and perfect lying in his arms. He wanted so much to pick her up and carry her to the bedroom, not to tuck her in but to show her how he felt about her. He had never forced himself on a woman nor ever tried to convince anyone to be with him after they had said "no".

As conflicted as he felt, he knew he was going to have to leave. He softly kissed her forehead, pulled one of the sofa pillows under her head and tenderly said good-bye then let *himself* out of Jonah's home, and *her* out of his life. He knew what his life would be like without Tauri Hill...empty.

Jonah sighed as he dropped his suitcase and garment bag on the front stoop as he placed his key in the front door of his home. He was glad everyone on the shoot cooperated and finished the project with all parties pleased with the results. The final edits would be done in the next couple of days then they would negotiate airtimes and perspective TV shows for their client to sponsor.

During the evening, fresh snow had fallen so he could not park in the garage. But there was a clear empty space curbside for parking in front of his condo.

When he opened his front door, he heard the television playing. Tauri must have fallen asleep while watching it. He hoped she was feeling better. He had not bothered to call ahead just in case he could not get a flight, or the flight was delayed.

Jonah left his bags near the door, walked over to the sofa, briefly watching Tauri all snug under the comforter and the television screen showing the screen saver pattern from the DVD player.

He smiled. She had probably fallen asleep watching, 'It's a Wonderful Life' again. He would leave her there until morning. She looked too peaceful to wake.

Chapter 8

It had been seventeen days, six hours and twenty-three minutes since Tauri had gone back to California. Eli looked at the clock on the dash of his car. *'Make that twenty-four minutes.'* She had not called, emailed, or texted him. Who was he kidding? She had made it perfectly clear she wasn't interested in a relationship. More importantly, he felt she did not want a relationship with *him*.

Eli shook himself and refocused on the road ahead. The day was clear but there was a weather report saying more snow was expected later that evening. He had passed the fifty-mile marker just outside of Chicago, letting him know he was less than an hour away from his childhood home in Springfield, Ill. His father, Edward, was a retired postal employee who had worked for over thirty-five years. His mother, Eliza, was a retired teacher but she still volunteered at the local high school from time to time as a tutor. He smiled as he remembered her saying she loved molding young minds.

When they were growing up, their parents were always arguing or not talking at all. Eli and his sister always thought it was strange that, now, his parents travelled a lot and were gone all the time. Maybe they were resigned to the fact they were stuck with each other.

During the holidays, they always stayed in the states to visit with family. Usually, after New Year, they went on a cruise or stayed at their timeshare in Key West, Florida throughout the winter. Whenever they would go away for long periods of time either he or his sister would check on the house.

This Christmas, they were supposed to be visiting Aunt Gloria, the one sister of his dad's, his mom actually got along with. Eli was glad his parents were out of town preparing for Christmas in Florida. Visiting his childhood home would give him time to get his head together. A change of scenery is what he needed.

Since Tauri left, he had been in a bad mood and did not feel like defending his reasons for not settling down, getting married and having children to his mother. He made a mental note to apologize for his moods to Iris and his team when they returned to work after the holidays.

He smiled when he thought of how little sleep he had gotten in the last few weeks. When he would wake in the middle of the night, his thoughts were of Tauri—not wanting to take her medicine, frowning at him for waking her, and making her eat or her begging him to stay with her when she was sweating out the flu. He pushed the pleasant memories aside then ordered himself to *'get past this.'* He had no choice because Tauri did not want him in her life. He was conflicted even with his *own* emotions.

Eli released a sigh as he took his exit. Fifteen minutes later, he pulled into the driveway of his parent's two-story brick home. Over the years, his father had renovated it—adding a sunroom, which enclosed the pool where he swam laps every day and a greenhouse to cater to his mother's love of flowers. He and his sister were always after them to sell it and buy something smaller, but his mother would ask where the grandchildren sleep when they came to visit doing the summer.

He sat and stared out through the windshield, then turned off the engine, opened the car door and looked around the neighborhood. A fresh white blanket of snow covered the neighbor's lawns. His parents and most of the neighbors paid a company to clear their street and driveways after a snow fall. For that he was grateful because he did not want his father getting injured while shoveling snow.

The surrounding, familiar landscape gave him a sense of comfort. The snow there in Springfield was always cleaner than in the city. Now that Tauri was gone, the snow made him feel cold. He had grown up here and knew how to deal with the gloom of the winter months. Even though his parents were not home, Eli always felt comfortable in his old room.

He walked to the trunk, pulled out his garment and overnight bag then headed to the front door. He put his key in the lock and opened the door. Suddenly he stopped. The alarm ping that gave thirty seconds to disarm had not sounded. All he heard was the chime signaling someone had just come in the front door.

He closed the door quietly and stood listening as he placed his bags on the floor. Maybe his dad forgot to arm the alarm. He immediately dismissed the thought because he knew his dad would never have forgotten.

Eli froze when he heard a noise coming from the kitchen. Slowly, he continued through the foyer into the formal living room toward the kitchen. The kitchen was another renovation his dad had done under strict directions from his mom.

"Mom? Dad? Are you guys here?" he called out.

Eli stopped and placed his hand on the cool dark brown granite top of the island that stood in the center of the floor. Suddenly he heard a giggle. He leaned over the island just enough to see over the other side. He gasped, then straightened.

"Damn," he whispered as he turned around and closed his eyes.

A hot wave of embarrassment covered his neck and face. He heard the giggle again. *Mom?* Then he heard his father's soft deep laughter. He could not believe it—his parents were making out on the kitchen floor! When he found his voice, Eli said in a scolding manner, not daring to turn around, "Mom? Dad? What are you guys doing?"

"Nothing anymore," his father mumbled. Eli could not believe he actually sounded disappointed.

"Are you alright dear?" Eli heard his father ask.

"Yes, thank you. Please help me up," his mother answered.

He heard feet shuffling and movement behind him.

"You can turn around now sweetie. I'm decent."

Eli heard the smile in her voice and he slowly turned to face his parents. His mother was smoothing her mussed silver and black hair, as she smiled at her husband, who was fussing with the skirt of her blue and purple flowered cotton dress.

His father smiled back as he stood next to her, his white dress shirt on the outside of his brown slacks. Edward reached out then pulled his wife of over thirty years to his side.

Eli stared at the two people who seemed like strangers.

"But I thought you two didn't... All those years. All those arguments. What's going on?"

His father cleared his throat, kissed Eliza's temple then released her.

"Come on son let's sit down. Your mother was about to pour us some coffee. I think you need a cup."

Moments later Eliza sat a cup of hot steaming coffee in front of Edward and Eli. Edward pulled a chair close to him and his mother sat across from Eli. Eliza placed her hand over her husband's right hand.

Now that the initial shock had receded, Eli looked at the two people he had known all his life in a new light.

Eli blinked when his mother apologized.

"We're sorry we shocked you, sweetie."

"I'm not," his father mumbled.

Eli had never heard his father mumble before—but today he heard him do it twice.

"Edward," his mother said in admonishment.

"Well, I'm not," the older man said and frowned over his coffee at Eli.

Eliza laughed and lightly tapped Edward's hand with her polished purple nails.

"Yes, you are Ed."

Eli tried to get an understanding.

"All those fights Sheila and I witnessed. A few times we thought you two were going to get a divorce."

Edward opened his mouth to speak but Eliza squeezed his hand and smiled.

"That was my fault," she said.

Edward took her hand in both of his and squeezed it.

"That statement is only partially true. In those days, I was a little out of control."

Becoming more confused, Eli asked, "could you guys please explain what you're talking about?"

"Eli, your father is a very passionate man."

Eli felt his face flush. He could not believe his parents—his mother—was talking to him like this.

"You see, Eli," his father added. "When I first saw your mother at a mutual friend's cookout, I knew I wanted her in my life and to be the mother of my children. For such a beautiful woman, she was incredibly shy. It took me a month to get her to go out with me and another month or two to get her to let me hold her hand in public, let alone kiss her."

Eli's eyes shifted from his father to his mother who was looking down at their joined hands. He had known his mother was somewhat quiet and shy, except with her immediate family. Eli was drawn back to his father's face when he spoke.

"It was so bad that when she finally consented to marry me, the only people in attendance were the judge and both sets of your grandparents."

His mother laughed and said, "I think our parents were watching us closely to see if the reason we wanted to marry the way we did was because I might have been pregnant."

Edward raised his thick black brow.

"That was definitely what your parents thought, but my parents knew me, so I wasn't worried."

His mother must have known what Eli was thinking. She touched his hand with her free one then smiled.

"Don't worry, sweetie. You were born two years after we were married."

'*Thank goodness*,' Eli thought. He did not want all of what he thought he knew to be too different or to think his grandparents thought ill of his mother was unthinkable.

"Eli, I'm sorry for what we put you and your sister through. We were so caught up in our own emotions, we did not take time to realize how our actions might shape your relationships throughout your lives. Sheila almost lost Mitchell. I knew it was because she had been afraid of what she saw us going through while you two were growing up."

The quiet in the kitchen seemed to hang in the air between the three of them.

He was sure his parents' relationship made a big impression on his dating life. He had worked so hard with Phyllis to make their relationship different from his parents. Now he was so relieved he had seen her true colors when he shared his vision of starting his own agency. Her vision did not line up with his. Phyllis had no confidence in him. Eli inhaled then slowly released it.

"Eli?"

Eli refocused on his mom.

"I'm sorry mom. What were you saying?"

Eliza placed her hand on his forearm.

"Are you alright, sweetie?"

He covered her hand with his own.

"Yes, I'm fine. It's just a lot to take in and seeing you two in a new light.

"I hope it's a good light," his mother beamed.

His father smiled and looked at Eli expectantly. Eli laughed and patted his mom's hand.

"Yes, mom. It's a very good light."

His mother stood.

"Good. I was about to prepare dinner. Is baked salmon okay?"

Eli grinned. His mother was an excellent cook and her baked salmon was the best he had ever tasted.

"Yes, ma'am."

While Eliza made herself busy with dinner, Eli and Edward remained at the table. Edward took a sip of his coffee.

"I know you thought we had left for Florida, son, but Lizzy wanted to wait another day before leaving. To what do we owe this visit? Did you change your mind and decide to join us?"

Eli looked down at his coffee as steam still rose from the cup.

"I needed to get away from the city for a while. I couldn't concentrate."

Edward looked back at Eliza. His mother broke the silence.

"Is the office already closed for the holidays, dear?"

Eli looked her way.

"Yes ma'am. We had a great year so everyone received an extra week off with pay."

"Iris must be ecstatic."

"That is an understatement. She was so happy she gave me a hug and a kiss."

His mother chuckled.

"She loves being with her family."

"Yes," Eli replied. She always says family is everything."

"As it should be," Edward said with a wink and took another sip of coffee. "The lineup is God, family, you, and everything else comes after. Keep that in your mind and you'll be okay."

"Yes sir. I didn't realize you wanted to spend time alone together. I can go back to the city. It is still early."

Eliza dried her hands on a dish cloth and walked over and stood in front of Eli. Concern covered her face.

"Nonsense, you can stay as long as you like. Eli, you're welcome to come with us. Sheila and Mitchell are off to Jamaica day after tomorrow and I don't want you to spend the holidays alone."

"I'll be fine, Mom. I may still go into the office and do some work. And Jonah invited me to go to California with him. I have options."

"I know you've heard this before, but life is more than work," Edward offered. "The best things in life are out there for you but they are not going to come to you."

Eliza gave her husband an adoring glance then looked back at Eli.

"Not always," she said. "Sometimes what you need is what you least expect. Don't let the opportunity pass you by."

She turned and looked at her husband of almost thirty-one years, and admitted, "I almost did. Besides, it's not good for man to be alone."

♡

After dinner, Eli's parents bundled up and went out for their daily walk. Eli thought it would be a good time to leave them to each other. They had a lot of years to catch up on.

As he drove back to Chicago, he smiled shaking his head.

"Wow. On the kitchen floor. Wow!"

He also thought about what his mother said about going after the best things in life.

Decision made. Eli hit the handsfree button on his steering wheel. At the beep he commanded, "call Jonah Hill."

Jonah answered on the second ring.

"Jonah Hill."

"Hey man, what day did you say you were leaving for Cali?"

♡

Chapter 9

Tauri woke up early in anticipation of a busy day. She'd done the cleaning the day before. Today was light dusting then making hundreds of cookies.

When Jonah arrived, he would pick-up the Christmas trees. It was already six days before Christmas and Jonah still had not told her what day he would arrive. There was a lot to be done before they could celebrate Christmas with their dad's sister, Aunt Ellie and her husband, John in Laguna Beach.

Tauri had not known her aunt growing up. Aunt Ellie was a child born to her grandfather, outside of his marriage, so their grandmother had never acknowledged her as part of the family.

When Tauri had been diagnosed with cancer, Jonah began searching for their aunt on social media and found her right there in California. It was during this time Jonah had chosen to move to Chicago.

He had been offered what he called a "once in a lifetime" position with one of the nation's most successful advertising agencies. It was always his plan to learn from the best but ultimately wanted to open his own agency. As Jonah's new life in Chicago began, Tauri's cancer diagnosis also began a different kind of change.

Jonah spent as much time as he could with Tauri during her treatments and recovery which meant commuting between Illinois and California. She was proud of him. He had come a long way from a high school kid who wanted to throw his life away by hanging out with the wrong crowd just to feel wanted. On top of everything else, and no matter how busy he was during the Christmas season, he always came home to help Tauri with her six days of Christmas.

Tauri looked around the living room and thought how blessed she and Jonah were. He was now doing well, and her two daycare centers were holding their own. Things had been tough for a while, with a few of the parents pulling their children because of the bad economy. She was able to talk some of the parents into applying for assistance to help with their childcare costs.

She was very proud of her handpicked teachers. They were not just babysitters but taught the children structure, social skills, teamwork as well as reading and writing. Each staff member also went through thorough background checks and continued education.

All of the teachers who were parents could enroll their children free of charge. She knew all the ladies loved children as much as they loved their jobs. On Christmas Eve, they would have their annual Christmas party. This year, she was able to gift each teacher with a sizeable bonus. Even with the economy struggling the way it was, she was not in the red, which she often worried would be the case. She never wanted to be forced to lay anyone off.

Tauri took a deep breath and continued her dusting. A bell sounded in the kitchen alerting her that another batch of cookies was ready to come out of the oven. Tauri quickly replaced the last item she had dusted—a picture of their parents, back on the mantle. She then hurriedly took the cookies out and put another prepared sheet into the oven.

As she closed the oven, she heard someone at the front door. She walked back into the living room, knowing it was Jonah. She was going to give him an ear full for not calling her. She stopped just inside the foyer. It *was* Jonah and he was not alone.

"Eli," she whispered.

"Hey Sis, look who I conned into coming with me. I didn't think you would mind the extra help," Jonah said with a big bright smile on his handsome face.

He walked over, carrying his garment and overnight bags, and kissed her on the cheek.

"Smells so good in here. I'll show Eli to the guest room."

Eli stood in the doorway, transfixed by the sight of the woman who had been literally haunting his dreams for the last three weeks. She stood looking at him in stunned silence. Her hair was secured in a messy bun on top of her head. Flour was smeared on her cheek.

Tauri Hill was standing there in her cropped green pants and cream top, staring at him with those big chocolate honey-brown eyes of hers. Eli smiled and greeted her.

"Hi, Tauri."

Slowly, he walked over and did as Jonah had—he kissed Tauri's cheek but allowed his lips to linger for moment.

"You smell good too," he whispered.

Tauri closed her eyes and breathed in his scent—one she remembered well. For goodness sake, the only place he had touched her was on her cheek, but she felt like he had touched her all over. *'Get a hold of yourself, girl,'* she told herself.

Eli had grown a thin chinstrap of a beard and an equally thin moustache. He looked even more handsome than he had looked almost a month ago. She tried hard to keep the quiver out of her voice, so she replaced it with irritation

"What are you doing here, Eli?"

He looked at her, a crooked smile on his lips.

"Jonah said this is a busy time of the year for you. I didn't have anything to do with two weeks off, so here I am. I came to help—so you won't get sick again."

She was not going to get caught up on him caring about her health. He had only looked after her as a favor to Jonah. And again, he had only come to help Jonah or so she told herself.

"Don't you have family?"

Tauri knew she sounded rude, but she was angry. She did not know if she was angry with Jonah for asking him to come or with Eli for accepting. Or even worse, was she angry with the way her mind and body reacted to Eli's presence? He was standing so close. All she had to do was put her head on his shoulder.

She blinked and couldn't believe what she thinking! She had to step back. He was too close, but her feet wouldn't move. Eli must have sensed what was going through her mind because he smiled again.

"Yes, but we were all together at Thanksgiving. During Christmas everyone mostly visits extended family."

When she did not answer, after a moment, he asked, "what's wrong Tauri? I wasn't on your list of things to do?"

Her mouth opened, then closed again. Jonah called over the second-floor railing, "come on, Eli. I'll show you to your room."

"Be right there," Eli called back.

He stared at Tauri a little while longer then stepped back, "We'll talk later."

He walked around her and went up the stairs carrying his small suitcase and garment bag.

Tauri stood where Eli had left her, wondering what was going on. She closed her eyes and inhaled. She had done a good job getting Eli out of her system for the last few weeks. At least she thought she had.

When she left Chicago, she told herself she would put him out of her head. He was a nice guy and the time they had together was precious. She would never forget it. But she had reconciled herself to the fact that there could never be anything between them.

The ting of the oven signaled that the next batch of cookies was done and ready to be taken out. She removed them and put in another batach, then she stopped and threw the oven mitt on the counter. *'Why did he have to come?'* How could she concentrate on all she had to get done by Christmas with Eli disrupting her thoughts? She was not entirely sure how she felt about him.

When she first returned from Chicago, it was hard for her to forget the memories of the way he had cared for her. How he had slept on the sofa and watched over her and convinced her to go to the doctor because he was worried about her. How could anyone forget that?

Tauri had managed to put memories away somewhere in her heart. She had decided a more intimate relationship between them would never work. She had written it off as *'it was nice and a good part of her life that I will always cherish.'* Now, all that had changed.

Just then, the hair stood up on the back of her neck.

"Tauri, are you alright?"

She turned and there Eli stood at the kitchen door, his brow wrinkled—those intense dark eyes looking at her—looking into her—trying to find his own answers.

She remembered that frown. She wanted to reach over and smooth the lines there, just as she had done before. *'My life is already complicated enough.'* After Oscar had left and she had recovered from the cancer treatments, she had purposely kept busy so she would not have any time to be lonely.

'I just don't have time for this,' she thought as she stared at Eli, who stood in front of her looking so good in a dark gray short sleeve pullover, form-fitting black jeans and red tennis shoes.

"Tauri?"

"Yes, I'm fine. I was just thinking about all the things I had to do today," she answered, half lying.

Eli walked further into the kitchen, frown intact, and stopped about two feet in front of her.

"What else do you have to do today," he asked after looking at all the cookies on the counter.

"For starters, I have to finish at least five dozen more cookies. Then I have to go with Jonah to get Christmas trees for the house and for the hall. *And,* I have to set up and decorate both trees. Jonah needs to pick up all of the donated toys at the collection locations we've set up and bring them back here to be wrapped."

The words tumbled out of her mouth. Eli's head was spinning. *'Why is she pushing herself so hard?'*

"And all that has to be done *today*?"

"Yes. All but the wrapping. Didn't Jonah tell you what to expect this week?"

"No. He just asked me if I wanted to have an interesting Christmas holiday. He told me to bring some jeans and tennis shoes."

At that moment, Jonah came down the stairs, stopping at the bottom step and looked into two pair of eyes.

"What?"

"Jonah, you didn't tell Eli about this week?" Tauri scolded.

Jonah grinned, and admitted, "I'm no fool. I need *help* Sis. Every year you run me into the ground with your six days of Christmas. I thought Eli would enjoy doing something different this year.

"What about *his* family, Jonah?"

Eli answered, "like I said before, we spent Thanksgiving together. We all gathered at my sister's home in New York. She and her husband are spending the holidays in Jamaica with his mother. My parents are visiting my aunt in Florida, so I'm good."

Eli's handsome face held an innocent smile. The oven timer pinged again. Tauri turned, grabbed the oven mitt from the counter, opened the oven, and pulled out a hot batch of chocolate chip cookies. She placed the hot sheet of cookies on the island and glared at the men standing in front of her.

"See," Jonah said as he grabbed a couple of the soft gooey cookies. "It's settled. Finally, after all these years, I have help! So, for *this* six days of Christmas, you won't be blowing up my phone to yell at me because I'm not going fast enough. You can yell at Eli, too."

Tauri put her hands on her hips, and quipped, "I only yell when you don't take care of business."

Jonah bit into another cookie.

"Tauri, you must have a hundred things on that list of yours for me to do."

She had to smile because her list for him had grown by one-third this year.

"You just make sure you get them all done."

Jonah grabbed two more cookies and offered them to Eli.

"Here you go, Bro. You better eat these until we can stop and pick up something."

"Where are you going first?" Eli asked as he munched.

Tauri picked up what looked to Eli like an ice cream scoop and dipped it into a bowl filled with cookie dough. She began to make rows in a previously prepared cookie sheet.

"Because you are here so late, I'm not going to go with you to pick up the trees," Tauri stated. "Just set them up and we can decorate them in the morning. The trees for the house and the senior center have already been paid for, netted and ready for pick-up."

Tauri put another batch of cookies in the oven.

"Eli and I will be fine, Sis. We couldn't help the flight being delayed for three hours," Jonah said trying to plead his case.

"Jonah," Tauri warned.

Jonah held up his hands in surrender.

"Okay, okay we're out of here. Where are the keys?"

"My purse."

Jonah told Eli that he never rented a car when he came home. His sister had a Chevy pick-up, she used mostly for all the charity work and a six-year-old BMW sedan—a present from Jonah. He had bought it with the commission he had earned from his first advertising campaign.

"Alright, we'll be back in a couple of hours. Do you need anything else while we're out?" Jonah said as he stopped at the door leading to the garage.

Tauri looked at the clock on the microwave and exhaled.

"No, but make sure they make a fresh cut on the bottoms of the trees and make sure there's plenty of water at the center of the stand."

"I know. I know."

Jonah turned again to leave but stopped.

"Tauri?"

When she looked up at him, he said, "thanks."

Jonah walked through the door with Eli on his heels. Tauri smiled and they were gone.

Chapter 10

Tauri plopped down in the nearest chair as soon as she heard the garage door roll down. She took a deep breath and exhaled, slowly, trying desperately to calm her body down. She'd wanted Eli to touch her. She wanted to touch his face. Just his face, to make sure she was not dreaming. *'What am I going to do?'*

Ever since she had returned from Chicago, Tauri had been trying to put Elijah Thornton out of her mind. She thought she had done just that until he walked through the front door.

She stretched out her hands in front of her. They were trembling.

"What is your problem girl," she asked herself, aloud.
She closed her eyes only to see an image of Eli's smiling face. Her eyes opened wide. *'I'm in trouble.'*

Tauri's touched her hair then her face. *'Oh, my goodness.'* Although Eli had seen her look her worst when he had taken care of her in Chicago, for some reason Tauri was embarrassed.

She rushed over to the phone on the counter next to the refrigerator and pressed the number one on the speed dial.

"Relax, Refresh, Feel Beautiful Hair Salon. This is Aly. May I help you?"

"Hi, Aly. May I come in today? Please, please, please?"

Alyson Harper had been her stylist for over ten years. Tauri had been one of her first clients when Aly moved from Georgia to California. From the first day, they had hit it off. Aly was also the first person Tauri told about her cancer diagnosis. Together they discussed how she should tell her brother and later, after the operation, what they would do about her hair once the treatments began.

Tauri's doctor had warned her that with the type of chemotherapy and radiation she would receive her hair would definitely fall out. The brochure she read about how to handle her diagnose suggested she could either get a short cut or shave off her hair. Either would give her a sense of control and it did.

She got a short cut at first. Then when her hair began to fall out at an alarming rate, after the initial treatment, she and Aly agreed to shave the rest. They had cried together after her treatments were completed. When her hair began to grow back, they celebrated. Now, almost three years later, her hair had grown long, thick and very healthy.

"Miss Santa," Alyson joked. "I thought you were too busy to come in."

"Something came up," Tauri told her, meaning someone came to town.

Tauri knew she would tell her friend about Eli eventually but not until she defined how she felt about him.

"Can you get me in?"

"One second, let me get my book."

Tauri listened on the line as she heard pages of Aly's appointment book rustling.

"Okay, I thought so. I had someone call and cancel on Friday or I have a two-hour slot for this afternoon."

Hope filled Tauri, she shouted, "YAY! I don't think it will take that long. What time?"

"If you can get here in a half hour with a tuna fish sub, chips and a diet coke, I'm all yours."
"I'll be there."

Eli and Jonah picked up the Christmas trees from the lot a couple of blocks from Tauri's house, and put them in the truck.

"Jonah? Why didn't you tell me about your sister's *six days of Christmas*?" Eli asked.

He shrugged his shoulders, and answered, "I didn't think you would come."

"I'm surprised. You've never seen me try to dodge work."

Jonah stopped behind a red sports car at a traffic light.

"You don't know Tauri. She's a mini Santa Claus and I'm her only elf. Today we do the trees while she bakes the cookies. Tomorrow we decorate the trees and pick up all the donated toys, wrap them and take them to the hall for the Christmas Eve party."

Jonah drove through the green light and turned right at the next corner.

"I don't think I'll tell you about the rest of the week. You might take a plane back to Chicago."

"Do you get to visit anyone while you're here?"

"Precisely, by the time I'm done with Tauri's list, my vacation is over."

"Why don't you just tell her no?"

"She's done too much for me. I could never say 'no' to her. Not too many people can tell Tauri 'no'. Her heart is too big. She couldn't hide it if she tried."

Jonah's shoulders sagged as he exhaled.

"Besides, I don't ever stay mad at her for long."

Eli knew what Jonah meant. When Tauri had been sick and got stubborn on him, he had gotten so mad when she did not want to do what he asked. When he bullied her and she complied, his anger vanished quickly.

Jonah pulled into a senior center and parked in front of a building named 'Hill Memorial Hall'.

"Any connection?" Eli asked.

"Yeah," Jonah replied. "Our grandfather donated the funds to build it after our grandmother passed away. Grandma volunteered here for years. She would come and read to the residents, bring snacks, make little lap quilts and just talk to them."

They both got out and walked to the back of the truck. Jonah reached in and picked up the end of one of the trees and dragged it out so Eli could get the other end.

"Could you grab the stand?" Jonah asked Eli.

Eli looked inside the far end of the truck bed and picked up the stand.

On the way into the hall, Jonah said, "the name used to be 'Hill Hall' until after Granddad's death, then it was changed to 'Hill Memorial Hall.'"

As Jonah reached for the door, it opened, and a small gray-haired elderly woman smiled at him.

"Hi, Jonah, sweetie. Merry Christmas!"

"Merry Christmas, Miss Mamie!"

Jonah leaned down and kissed her cheek and made introductions.

"Miss Mamie, this is my friend and colleague, Elijah Thornton, from Chicago. Eli—Miss Mamie Carlton."

"Merry Christmas, Elijah. And welcome to Hill Memorial Hall," she said with a bright smile.

He nodded because his hands were full.

"Nice to meet you, Miss Mamie."

"Come on in. The girls are having their afternoon aerobics class. Just put the tree in the clearing by the fireplace."

When they were inside and had put the tree in its place, they stood back, looking to make sure it was centered. Miss Mamie walked in and stood beside them.

"You young men did a good job. Where is Tauri? Isn't she going to decorate it today?"

"No ma'am," Jonah explained. "She's making all those cookies today and she has some other things going. We'll be back here in the morning to decorate it."

Mammie nodded and turned to Eli.

"Are you coming back tomorrow, too, young man?"

"Yes ma'am. I'll be back." Eli grinned down at her. Miss Mamie reminded him of his granny.

The aerobics class session must have ended because they were now surrounded by elderly ladies of varying nationalities, hair colors and sizes. All were shorter than Jonah and Eli.

It seemed to Eli they all started talking at the same time—everyone welcoming Jonah and saying friendly "hellos" to Eli. In return, Jonah offered a genuine, heartwarming smile and gave hugs and introductions, to Eli, as he progressed through the gathering of ladies.

"Where's Tauri, Jonah?" a cute plump curly haired woman Eli remembered being introduced as Doris, asked as she held onto Jonah's elbow. Miss Mamie spoke before Jonah had a chance.

"She's making cookies, Doris. You know, for the Christmas tins she gives us every year?"

"Yes, I remember, like last year. I think I received some chocolate chip and some sugar cookies."

Doris looked at Eli, while holding on to Jonah's arm.

"Tauri doesn't really put sugar in the cookies because she knows some of us can't have it. She makes sure we all get something."

The rest of the group agreed. Different people chimed in.

"She's a good girl."

Another agreed, "yes, she sure is. She is always nice to us and asks about my great grandkids."

"Mine too," another said.

"She is so much like her grandmother. Always caring for the well-being of others," Miss Mamie added.

Jonah smiled down at all of the ladies.

"Yes, ma'am, Miss Mamie, she always has. Well, we must be going. We've got a couple more stops to make. See you all tomorrow!"

Miss Mammie smiled.

"Tell Tauri we all said hi and we'll be waiting tomorrow to trim the tree."

"Yes ma'am. I will." Jonah said as he waved goodbye.

Eli smiled down at the cheery group of grandmothers and great grandmothers.

"It was an honor to meet all of you young ladies."

A big "ahhh" chorused through the room which was followed by a couple of giggles.

"Make sure you bring him back tomorrow, Jonah," one of the ladies said.

Both men grinned. Jonah replied, "Yes ma'am. See you tomorrow. Have a good night."

When they reached the truck, Eli said, "They're a nice group of ladies."

Jonah gave Eli a sidelong glance as they both climbed into the cab of the truck.

"Don't be fooled. They were sizing you up for one of their granddaughters or grandnieces. I wouldn't be surprised if some of them aren't present tomorrow when we come back to trim the tree."

Eli smiled and shook his head. *'This is turning out to be one interesting Christmas vacation.'*

As promised Tauri, arrived at *Relax, Refresh, Feel Beautiful Hair Salon* with a footlong tuna fish sandwich on wheat, a bag of salt and vinegar chips, a diet coke and a variety of freshly baked cookies.

Aly was using a flat iron on Tamika Olsen's shoulder length hair.

"Hey girl! Right on time. I'm almost finished."

Tamika looked up and smiled at Tauri in the mirror.

"Hi Tauri. How have you been?"

"Hi, Mika!"

Tauri smiled back as she placed the food and drink on a nearby table.

"I've been doing spectacular. You know this is my time of year."

Tamika attended Tauri's church and worked with the hospitality ministry. She was a beautiful person inside and out. Tauri knew Mika was in her mid-forties but she looked ten years younger. She was one of the people who had prayed for and encouraged Tauri when she was going through cancer treatments. When Mika asked how she was doing, Tauri knew it was not a casual greeting. Tauri was always truthful about her health with her. Mika was naturally upbeat, caring and genuinely kind.

Mika smiled, and asked, "and how is poor Jonah holding up with your Six Days of Christmas?"

"He's young, he'll survive. He just arrived this morning and is out picking and setting up Christmas trees."

"All done Mika," Aly announce and patted Mika's shoulders and turned the salon chair around.

Mika stood, hugged Tauri and kissed her cheek.

"Thank you!" Mika told Ali before turning and looking in the mirror. My hair looks fabulous as always."

Then she turned to look at Tauri.

"You look so good, Tauri."

"Why thank you. Mika!"

"It's true," Mika went on. "The Lord's blessings are all over you. Have you thought about attending the breast cancer survivor's meeting we talked about, and sharing your testimony?"

"Yes, I have. I think I will put it on my calendar for either February or March. It was a scary time and I still need to wait a little while before I can share it with anyone."

"I understand, but sometimes the scary things in life are what keeps us strong or makes us stronger."

"You're right Mika. How did you get so wise?"

"Living girl. Just living!"

Mika squeezed Tauri's arms then dropped her hands. She retrieved her purse from the cubby under the station counter then hugged and kissed Aly on the cheek.

"Thank you, girls," Mika said to both. "I have to get some last-minute shopping done. Aly, I sent your payment and a little gift via electronic funds transfer."

Aly smiled.

"Thank you, Mika, and Merry Christmas. I'll see you right before the New Year."

"Okay. Bye!"

And Mika was gone.

Tauri looked around.

"Wow, this place is empty."

Aly had four hair stylist's stations, one manicurist/pedicurist station and one station for the barber that came in twice a week.

"Yes. Two of the ladies took early morning appointments and one is on vacation. I only have one more person after you leave. Christmas week is busy for everyone."

"I guess so," Tauri agreed and moved the bag of food and the drink from the table to the station. "Well, sit and eat your food so you'll have energy for the rest of your day."

"Alright. Let me wash my hands."

Aly came back, said a short prayer then began to eat.

"I see you bought me some cookies."

"Yes," Tauri replied and held up the plastic sandwich bag, "this is a sampler."

Aly smiled, and said, "thank you. Did you finish baking?"

"No, I have about three dozen more to make. I'll do them when I get back."

Aly shook her head.

"Girl, I don't know how you do it."

"It's only once a year."

"So why the change?

Tauri looked away.

"What?"

Aly wiped her mouth then re-wrapped the remaining sandwich and placed it back in the bag along with the cookies.

"Tauri. You know what I'm talking about."

They stared at each other for a moment.

"Okay. Jonah brought someone home with him."

Aly froze in the process of standing.

"Not your nurse?"

Tauri nodded.

Aly gasped then placed her hands over her mouth, her eyes wide.

"Oh, my goodness!"

When Aly could speak again, she asked, "really, you mean Jonah's co-worker? Your nurse while you were sick in Chicago?"

Tauri nodded, then frowned.

"Yes. And I think I'm in trouble."

Aly picked up her bag with her sandwich and chips.

"Come on back to the shampoo bowl."

She raised up her lunch bag.

"I'll put this in the fridge for dinner."

Tauri walked to the back of the salon and sat in the chair in front of the first shampoo bowl. She was not sure she should voice her feelings about Eli because she was trying hard not to think about them. She trusted Aly not to pass on their conversation and whatever they shared would be held in confidence. Some stylists were like therapists and most people spoke freely while they were getting pampered.

"Okay, let me grab a cape and a towel then we'll be ready."

Toweled and caped, Aly laid Tauri back over the shampoo bowl and lifted her feet up on the footrest. Aly shampooed and massaged Tauri's scalp then applied a conditioner and placed her under the dryer for twenty minutes. Afterwards, Aly rinsed her hair then bought her back over to the station.

"Now, are you interested in a cut or just a trim?" Aly asked Tauri while looking at her reflection in the mirror.

"A cut, I think. I'll let you decide."

Aly smiled.

"That could be dangerous."

They both laughed.

Aly grabbed her electronic tablet then scrolled through her portfolio. After every new style she had done for a client, she asked if she could take a picture for her files. She scanned through the section on hairstyles until she saw the style she was looking for. Then she handed the tablet to Tauri.

"This one is perfect for you. This is called a graduated bob. It is versatile. You can place the part on either side or in the middle. I'll have the front frame your face. You can throw some curls in it or not. Your hair came back so thick and healthy, the cut would look fabulous and very sexy," Ali said wiggling her eyebrows.

Tauri giggled.

"I like it. Let's do it."

Aly started cutting.

"So, what is the co-worker, nurse's name again?"

"Elijah Thornton. Eli for short."

"How long is he staying?"

"I don't know. Jonah will leave after the New Year but I'm sure Eli will probably leave after Christmas."

"You sound like you're not too pleased with that idea."

Tauri was quiet for a moment then looked away from Aly's eyes in the mirror.

"It doesn't matter Aly. Long distance relationships..."

"So, you've already thought about it. He has really made an impression on you."

Tauri's eyes met Aly's in the mirror.

"Don't get me wrong," Tauri said. "He's a sweet guy when he's not bossy. Very caring and considerate and..."

Aly cut her off.

"And handsome?"

Tauri smiled, and answered, "yes, and handsome. If you can make it to the Christmas party, you'll get to meet him."

"Girl, he is *not* Oliver."

"Oscar."

"Whatever. That A-hole never cared about anyone but himself. I think you were just arm candy to him; someone to show off to his friends and family."

Aly held up her rat tail comb.

"When you became ill and he ran in the opposite direction—well that did it for me! Did he ever call you again?"

"Just once to tell me he had been transferred to Dallas."

"They should have transferred his behind to Alaska," Aly said laughing. "Better yet, Antarctica. They have oil there, don't they?"

By now Tauri was laughing so hard, Aly had to stop cutting her hair.

"Girl, stop!" She pleaded between breaths. "He was a jerk, but I forgave him a long time ago."

"You forgave him, but you haven't forgotten what he did to you. He shattered your trust and now you're afraid to allow anyone else to get close to you. You're just making excuses."

"Aly, you don't even know him."

"No, but Jonah does."

Tauri stared at Aly in the mirror.

"Do you think in a million years Jonah would have asked just anyone to look in on his sick sister while he was out of town on business? Or would ask just some guy he didn't trust to come and stay in your home for the holidays? Tauri, you need to be happy again. I know all of this charity work you do is fulfilling, but having someone to share it with, right by your side..."

"I'll think about it," Tauri she said with consideration.

But Aly didn't let up.

"Just live. Let it happen—whatever it is. I think you'll regret it if you let Eli get away from you. Besides, I know you want some little Tauris running around some day."

Tauri looked at Aly's reflection, in surprise.

Aly laughed then added, "or some little Elis."

They stared at each other then burst into laughter.

When Tauri caught her breath, she said, "Aly, you are so messy."

"I'm just making you think of the possibilities."

Minutes later, Jonah and Eli pulled into the parking lot of a small building with the name *'Best Sandwiches in Town'* on the marque. The small eating area was filled with teenagers of various ages, all chatting and laughing.

"Hi, Jonah!" one of the young ladies yelled from behind the counter.

Jonah grinned as the younger woman came around the counter and grabbed her in a big hug. She stood about a head shorter than Jonah, her dark hair pulled back into a tight bun, accenting a beautiful heart shaped caramel colored face. When she stepped back, she pulled down on the top of her navy-blue uniform. Her gold name tag read, Manager on Duty, Mona Ericson.

Jonah smiled down and greeted her; "hi Mona. How's it going?"

"Good. When did you get in?"

"Today. Can you believe Tauri has me working already?"

Mona tapped her watch, saying, "yeah, but you are a day late."

Jonah hung his head then looked back up.

"Guilty. Mona Lisa Ericson, this is my friend and co-worker Eli Thornton. Eli, Mona."

Mona held out her hand.

"It's a pleasure to meet you, Eli."

Eli took her hand.

"Likewise, Mona."

"You two hungry?"

"Yes, but nothing heavy," Jonah answered. "We have two more stops to make and I'm sure Tauri is going to have dinner ready in a few hours."

"Tauri was in here yesterday looking for toy donations. I gave her what I had but more have come in since then. I'll get them from the back while you place your order."

"Thank you, Mona."

Jonah and Eli found a small table in a corner of the restaurant. Eli ordered a shredded beef sandwich with cheddar cheese and cabbage. Jonah ordered a chicken barbecue sandwich; both orders came with fries and a soda. Within minutes their meals were delivered to their table.

Eli bit into his sandwich then moaned. He had not eaten since before they boarded the plane this morning.

"This is pretty good," he said, around a mouth full of sandwich.

Jonah nodded as he chewed.

"The secret's in the delicious, homemade bread. When I was in school, I was the bread maker until Tauri made me get a better paying job at a restaurant down the street."

When they finished their meal, Mona came over carrying the rest of the donated toys.

Here you are Jonah. These are the last of them. If we get more, I'll give them out to our customers as they come in."

"Thanks, Mona."

Jonah took some of the toys from Mona then gave them to Eli.

"Take these, Bro. I'll be right out."

"Got it. It was a pleasure, Mona, and my sandwich was amazing."

"Thank you, Eli. It's all in the bread and it was good to meet you also. I hope you enjoy your stay and Merry Christmas!"

Eli smiled.

"I will, thank you."

He nodded, then walked out of the door. The pair watched Eli leave before Mona asked Jonah, "did you know LaShelle worked at the northern center?"

Jonah was quiet for a moment.

"Yes, Tauri told me. How is she?"

Mona sighed; "she's living if that's what you mean. She smiles but I can tell her spirit is sad."

She handed Jonah the rest of the toys then touched his arm.

"Talk to her, Jonah."

This time, Jonah sighed; "I'll think about it."

He kissed her cheek.

"I've got to go. Probably see you again before I head out."

A short while later, Jonah pulled into the parking lot of the first daycare center.

"So, this is one of Tauri's daycare centers," Eli stated.

"Yes. This is what Tauri calls her southern center and the northern one is near our home on the other end of town. She doesn't put live trees in the centers. It's safer to buy artificial ones. The trees are stored in the storage room until I get in to put them together."

Jonah parked and they both climbed out and walked toward the entrance.

"I should have arrived on Saturday or Sunday..." Jonah said as they walked. "...when the centers are closed, but I needed a day of rest before I came."

"Does this bother you every year? All the things Tauri has you doing?"

"Nah. I like to complain just to get a rise out of her. Sometimes around the holidays, she misses our parents and gets melancholy. I'd rather see her upset with me; which doesn't last long, than to see her sad when I leave her here and go back to Chicago."

Eli was silent. He did not like the thought of Tauri being sad. Jonah looked at his watch.

"This is the beginning of their two-hour nap time. If we're lucky, everyone will be in their specific areas getting ready for their quiet time. Hopefully, there won't be any curious little eyes wanting to know what we're doing."

Jonah opened the door to a bright cheerful reception area. Brightly painted yellows, oranges, greens, and blues were artfully splattered on all the walls. Oversized letters and numbers were also displayed haphazardly over the paint.

A round faced, African American young woman at the front desk looked up from her computer screen and smiled. Her dark eyes grew wide with excitement as recognition registered.

"Jonah!"

She popped up from her chair and came around the desk with her arms stretched out.

"Hi Deja!" Jonah beamed.

Her head barely reached his shoulders. Jonah scooped her up and swung her around. When he put her down, they stood and grinned at each other.

"I thought you were supposed to be here this last weekend."

"I was delayed."

Jonah turned towards Eli.

"Deja this is my friend and co-worker Eli Thornton. Eli this is Dejanice Austin, an old friend. We went to high school together. We all call her Deja."

Eli smiled and stretched out his hand.

"It is nice to meet you, Deja."

"It's nice to meet you too, Eli."

She shook his hand then asked Jonah, "how long are you going to be in town, Jonah?"

"Until New Year's Day. Eli will probably go back as soon as he can after he sees all the things Tauri has on her list."

Deja laughed, and admitted, "we all love it though. She makes the season so special for all of us; especially all the children. Is she coming in today?"

"No," Jonah told her. "We'll be back sometime tomorrow, probably before lunch or during naptime."

Deja nodded.

"Well, we better get going, before she starts calling—trying to find us."

"Okay, I'll buzz you in. Let's have dinner before you go back."

"Let me know when."

"I will."

A loud buzzer sounded, and Jonah pushed open a door.

"Thanks De."

Eli followed Jonah down a hallway with glass windows on both sides. He saw rooms filled with little pallets aligned in neat rows. Each one contained a sleeping little body covered with various colorful blankets and quilts. Under low light, soft music played as three teachers monitored them from different vantage points around the room. Jonah waved at them as they walked.

When they reached the end of the hall, Jonah turned right into a large room with brightly colored carpet. Again, oversized letters and numbers decorated the walls. A cork board in the corner of the room held a collection of art in crayon and finger paints, created with tiny hands in an array of bright colors. To Eli, the room felt vibrant and alive. A perfect place for young minds to develop.

"Did Tauri decorate this facility herself?"

"Yes. She and her director, Claire, decorated both locations."

Jonah pulled a key ring from his pocket, found the key he was looking for, and opened a door in the middle of one of the walls.

"It looks like Claire is at the northern location today."

He walked in and disappeared.

"Here we are," Eli heard him say. "Right where I left it."

Jonah walked out carrying an oblong box with a picture of a Christmas tree on the side.

"This should only take a few minutes."

True to his word, Eli and Jonah were on their way to the northern facility inside of thirty minutes.

When they arrived at the northern location, the receptionist greeted Jonah in almost the same manner as Deja had at the southern facility. Jonah introduced the bubbly young woman as Deborah to Eli. When the introductions were made, Deborah phoned Claire to come up front.

Deborah buzzed them in through the door. On the other side was a petite Latina with a dimpled smile and ebony curls that bounced around her shoulders and fell in a waterfall down her back.

"Jonah, hi! I was wondering when I would see you." Jonah grabbed her in a big bear hug and picked her up off of the floor. He kissed her on the cheek before setting her on her feet and letting her go.

They both smiled as they faced Eli.

"Eli, this is Mrs. Claire Torres. She's Tauri's director of operations for both facilities. She held down the fort when Tauri got sick in Chicago. Claire, this is Eli Thornton. He nursed Tauri back to health."

"It is a pleasure to finally meet you," Eli said with a toothy smile. "You made her recovery so much easier. She didn't have to worry about anything back here."

"Hola. Elijah. So, you're the nurse?"

"I guess you could call me that."

"Thank you for taking care of my friend. We missed her around here, but we knew she was in good hands."

"You're welcome."

Claire smiled at Eli before she turned back to Jonah.

"I pulled the tree out and put it in the activity room."

"You didn't have to do that," Jonah said.

"Tauri called me earlier and told me you would be over this afternoon and I had some time. No biggie and I know Tauri. I think your list grew from last year."

"Yes, but I don't mind because I came prepared this year," Jonah said pointing to Eli. "Tauri can be militant this time of year." Jonah added.

"Giving back, is a need to her, and a gift to others. So many people were there when she needed them."

They were all quiet for a moment. Claire cleared her throat.

"Well, I better get back to work. I'll be in my office if you need anything."

Eli thought it right to thank Claire, personally.

"Thanks, Claire."

"No problem. Nice to meet you, Eli."

"Same here, Claire."

Eli helped Jonah unbox and assemble the eight-foot artificial tree. They both turned when they heard a sound behind them. In the doorway stood a little boy, a little over three feet tall with big brown eyes and a neat haircut.

"It's looks like someone's not sleepy today," Eli said.

"Hey, buddy," Jonah smiled. "What are you doing up?"

"I don't take long naps anymore. I'm five. I'm in kindergarten."

"Yeah? What's your name?"

"Jerimiah."

"Hi Jerimiah. My name is Jonah, and this is Eli."

Eli said, "hi."

"Hi," Jerimiah said as he waved his hand. "Can I be your helper?"

"Sure. We can use two more hands."

"Mrs. Summers said I am a good helper."

Jerimiah smiled, then came into the room and picked up the assembled tree stand. Eli and Jonah looked at each other as the young boy struggled with the metal stand. Slowly, he carried it over then placed it on the floor beneath a large window.

Eli and Jonah carried over the huge tree and without any prompting, Jerimiah guided the plastic bark of the tree into the hole in the center of the stand. The tree went in with a thump.

"How did you know the tree bark went into the stand like that?"

The young man shrugged his small shoulders.

"I just did."

Eli and Jonah busied themselves with straightening the branches until it resembled the picture of the tree on the box. When they finished, the three of them stood and looked at their handy work.

"Good job." Eli said.

"Well I better go back. Bye, Jonah! Bye, Eli!"

Jerimiah waved as he left the room.

"Bye, Jerimiah," Eli said as he waved. "Thanks for your help."

Jonah began to fold the tree box then stopped when he heard a female voice in the hallway.

"Jerimiah, there you are. I've been looking all over for you."

"I helped put up the tree."

"That's good. All right now, get back in the room and be quiet."

"Okay."

Moments later, a slim African American woman walked into the room. She stopped just short of where the tree stood. She looked at the tree, then at Jonah, his face showing no expression.

"Hello, Jonah."

Her greeting was hopeful but she showed no signs of offering Jonah a hug, nor did he look as though he expected one.

"Hello, LaShelle."

"How have you been?"

"Good. Working. Been busy."

She turned to Eli.

"Hello. My name is LaShelle Kenyon."

She offered her hand.

Eli looked from Jonah to LaShelle, then at her outstretched hand. He took her hand and held it gently.

"Yes, my name is Elijah Thornton, but my friends call me Eli."

LaShelle's lips formed a smile but it did not reach her eyes. Eli released her hand.

"Pleased to meet you, Eli."

"Likewise."

Jonah walked over to the storage room with the folded box, opened the door and placed it inside. He turned and faced Eli and LaShelle.

"Tauri will be back tomorrow to decorate the tree. Eli, we'd better get back."

LaShelle looked down at her folded hands.

"It was nice to meet you," Eli said.

"Yes. Thank you, Eli and you also."

She looked at Jonah then turned and walked out of the room.

Eli had never seen Jonah treat anyone in such a manner, especially a woman. Jonah lead the way down the hall to the front of the building. They waved at Claire as they passed her office. When they arrived at the SUV, Eli stopped Jonah before he opened the driver's side door.

"Jonah, what was that about?"

Jonah looked over at Eli, opened the vehicle door and climbed in. Eli did the same. Jonah started the engine, then said, "I loved her once, but she loved someone else."

He put the truck in gear the head for home.

Chapter 11

Jonah and Eli had been gone for almost three and a half hours. Tauri was careful to call only once, to ask Jonah to pick up wine if they wanted any for dinner. She had been able to have Aly do a quick job on her hair and was pleased with the results. She had even made it back in time to finish the last few dozen cookies and start dinner.

She stood for a moment and remembered her conversation with Aly. *'Let it happen,'* she had said. In truth, she had not realized how much she missed him until she had talked about him in detail with Aly.

This was the first time she had thought of a possible future with Eli and what that would look like. She also had to be honest with herself because Tauri had daydreamed from time to time while at work. She wondered what it be like to be a mother, especially when she visited the nursery.

Sometimes she would step into relieve one of her caregivers for lunch or a break or when someone called in sick. It was always her pleasure to help and be involved with those young lives. The thought of having a family with Eli had also never entered her mind until today.

If she did let it happen, what would be the result? They could end up trying to make the trips back and forth from Chicago to California to spend time with each other. The unknown possibilities only lead to thinking in terms of her relationship to Oscar. One of her projects would require extra work or his job might demand he work or travel on the weekend, putting a strain on their relationship. She expected he would want her complete attention and have her put aside her ambitions to make things work. Her ever thinking mind concluded it would never work.

Tauri jumped when she heard the garage door open and in both of them marched with tree in hand. Eli and Jonah placed the unloaded tree in front of the plate glass window in the family room. They stood back and looked at their handy work.

"Looks good," Eli said, standing beside Jonah.

"Not yet, just wait until Tauri gets through with it. We'll probably decorate it after dinner."

They went back outside to unload the toys they had picked up. After taking the toys upstairs to an empty bedroom, they walked into the kitchen, found it empty and continued into the dining room.

The round glass table was set for three. Crystal wine glasses and water goblets sat next to the palm printed china. "Please wash up. Dinner is ready."

They both turned at the sound of Tauri's voice.

She stood in the space between the dining room and the kitchen. The new hair cut framed her face and accented her long neck. She wore a gold zippered sweater with small raised circle designs around the neck and a pair of black Capri pants with a pair of black mule sandals on her feet.

"I like the hair, Sis. I'll be right back," Jonah said over his shoulder as he raced up the stairs.

Eli drank in the site of her. She absolutely glowed. It was as if he were frozen where he stood.

"You look nice."

Tauri stared back.

"Thank you."

She could tell he wanted to touch her. He took a step toward her. Tauri's eyes widened as her breathing quickened. She could not let him touch her. He kept walking then stopped right in front of her, almost touching. He smelled of cologne and spruce. It overwhelmed her. She finally found her voice.

"The bathroom is off the foyer to the right. You can wash up in there."

"I know what you're doing, Tauri. No use in trying to prolong it. It's going to happen."

When she gasped, he smiled then walked toward the bathroom.

Tauri closed her eyes and realized what he said was probably true, but she was going to fight it. She did not want to start a relationship with him, then have him walk away when he wasn't getting enough attention.

Oscar had always complained that she did not spend enough time with him and always questioned their relationship. When he had experienced the first six days of Christmas, she knew he was getting close to being done.

It really all came to an end on Christmas Eve when she told him about the results of a mammogram taken a few days earlier. He said he could not handle it and he was sorry then abruptly left.

She did not want to go through that pain again. So, for the last four years, Tauri had purposely pushed relationships aside and busied herself to keep those memories at bay.

Eli was disrupting those plans. He was pushing his way in and she was weakening even though she knew she should not. When he experienced the next couple of days, he would run back to Chicago and not look back.

She had a demanding schedule and she was going to keep it. That thought seemed to give her more courage. She straightened her shoulders, went to the stove and began spooning their dinner into bowls to be placed on the table.

The two men appeared in the doorway almost at the same time. Tauri looked up from what she was doing and stared at them staring at her.

"Well, don't just stand there. Help me put the food on the table."

Dutifully, they sprang into action. When everything was done to Tauri's satisfaction, they all sat. Eli helped Tauri with her chair.

"Everything looks good, Tauri," Eli said as his eyes scanned the dinner table.

Tauri cooked baked pork chops, collard greens, corn on the cob, candied yams, green beans, and cornbread. Jonah had asked Eli to pick a wine. He selected a smooth, buttery Chardonnay.

"And it will all taste good, too," Jonah said enthusiastically.

"Thank you," Tauri said to both compliments. "Jonah, could you please say grace?"

He did as she requested, and they began their meal.

"How did the delivery go at the hall?" Tauri asked, as the dishes were passed around the table.

"Miss Mamie and the ladies were in rare form."

"You know they love you, Jonah." Tauri said with a smile.

"Yeah, right. They love me as a new grandson."

Tauri laughed and her face lit up. Eli sipped on his glass of wine, gasped and began coughing. They both looked at him.

"Are you ok," Jonah asked.

"Eli?" Tauri said, concern written all over her beautiful face.

Eli grabbed his napkin and covered his mouth as the coughing subsided. He nodded with his watering eyes, not being able to speak yet. It was the first time he had heard Tauri laugh. He was not prepared for what it did to his senses. He took a little extra time to get his composure, keeping the napkin to his mouth.

"Are you sure?" Tauri said, the frown still in place.

"Yes," Eli said clearing his throat, then drinking a big gulp of cold water. "I'm fine. The wine went down the wrong way. Please continue."

"If you're sure," Tauri said.

Eli nodded.

"Miss Mamie has been trying to find Jonah a good woman for years," Tauri said her brow was still creased, but laughter was in her words.

"Don't laugh Tauri. I think they have their eyes on you as well."

"Miss Mamie and I've already had that talk."

"What talk is that?" Eli asked then looked closely at her.

Tauri glanced at Eli then looked down at her plate.

"I don't need any more complications in my life right now."

She looked up right into Eli's eyes.

"My charity work and day care centers are more important to me than a relationship. I don't want to jeopardize anything I have accomplished right now."

"You wouldn't have to compromise anything if you had the right man in your life—one who fully supported what you are doing."

"That kind of man is hard to find," Tauri said, lifting her chin just a little.

"I don't think you've looked hard enough."

Tauri narrowed her eyes, anger flashed in them. Jonah recognized the spark of war in Tauri's eyes and decided to change the subject.

"I hate to interrupt such an interesting topic, but we need to finish up here and get the tree decorated. I want to visit some people this evening because I don't know if I'm going to get another chance while we're here."

Both Eli and Tauri looked at Jonah as if they had forgotten he was at the table. After a moment, Eli looked at Tauri.

"We can finish this discussion another time."

As they ate, the conversation drifted from the weather, to the tree lot, and the old friends Jonah had seen while they were out. Jonah and Eli both commented on not missing the winter in Chicago.

"Let's do the tree," Jonah said.

Tauri cleared her throat.

"We still have dessert."

Jonah stood with his plate in hand.

"I'll eat it later."

"Leave it, Jonah I'll clean up. You can start bringing in the decorations from the garage," Tauri said in her big sister voice.

"I can live with that."

"I'll help with the cleanup," Eli said.

"Thanks," Jonah said then he was gone.

Tauri frowned, "You don't have to, Eli. It'll only take a min..."

"I do have to," Eli said in a tone that expected no further argument.

When she heard the door leading to the garage close, Tauri's frowned deepened as she stood with her plate in her hand.

"You are still very pushy."

"And you're still very stubborn."

A scowl creased his brow when he added, "You're well, aren't you?"

"Yes," she said answering both questions.

She just stood and stared at him, thinking back to when he had taken care of her in Chicago.

"For goodness sake Eli, I only had the flu. It doesn't last forever."

Heat creeped up her neck as her immediate thoughts of Eli's care in her recovery played in her mind. She turned away before he could sense her emotions and walked into the kitchen.

Eli smiled. He saw her eyes soften as she was probably remembering the same thing he was. He would never forget the feeling he felt—waking up with her in his arms. He picked up his plate and stacked it on top of Jonah's, then grabbed the stemware and followed Tauri into the kitchen.

She did not have to look around to know that Eli was standing right behind her. Tauri finished rinsing the plate in her hand, then turned around and brushed against his hard form. He seemed to ignore her sharp intake of breath. He reached around her with both arms and placed the plates and stemware in the sink, then placed both hands on the edge of the sink. effectively pinning her in.

"You smell good. Did I tell you that already today?"

"Yes, Eli."

She tried to look around him to see if Jonah was back yet. "Why are you here?"

"Your hair," he deflected. "The new cut looks nice."

"Thanks. Answer my question," she insisted.

She swallowed twice when Eli said, "I need another kiss."

"That was a mistake."

"All six times?"

"Eli, this will never work. You have your work, which you are very good at, and I have mine. I have no intention of having my work take a back seat to my personal life."

Eli's was sullen when he told her, "Tauri, you don't know me that well, but I would never ask you to leave something which meant so much to you."

Tauri searched his face to see if she could tell if he was lying to her. Somehow, something in his eyes made her believe he was telling the truth.

The door leading to the garage opened and then slammed shut again. Eli did not move. Tauri pushed against his chest. Eli kept his eyes on her face.

The door opened again. Jonah yelled, "A little help, please!"

"Be right there," Eli yelled over his shoulder then turned back and said to Tauri, "I'll still need that kiss."

"If I do then will you go help Jonah?"

He nodded.

"Okay."

He moved in slowly not moving his hands from the sink. His lips felt like a feather brushed across her lips. Then he walked out to help Jonah.

Tauri turned around and faced the sink and hung her head. She had to work to slow her breathing, little by little. Her hands were trembling. Truth be told, her entire body was trembling. *'Get a hold of yourself, girl'*, she reminded herself. *'You know Eli. He is an honorable man. He wouldn't do anything you didn't want him to do.'*

She *did* want more of a kiss than he had just left her with. She was definitely struggling with herself. Her mind was saying one thing, but her body wanted his touch. Her body wanted to throw caution out the window.

She lifted her head as a thought struck her. Did she want him to do whatever he wanted to do? What would that say about the type of person she was? What kind of relationship would they have? He would be in Chicago—she would be here in California. She couldn't stand the thought.

It had taken her all this time, from the end of November until two minutes before he walked through her door, to get him out of her system. He had touched her so carefully and tenderly when she was sick. Tauri closed her eyes to the fact that she missed it. She had missed him. Now that he was here, she did not know how to feel or even admit she was fearful of her feelings.

"Tauri, are you done yet?" Jonah yelled from the family room.

She jumped with a start.

"Almost," she yelled back. "I'll be there as soon as I can. Could you please check the water level again before you start?"

"I always do, Sis."

Chapter 12

An hour later Tauri stood back, looked at the tree and smiled as Jonah placed the last crimson ornament on one of the lower branches. *'Perfect.'*

The tree was decorated in record time—probably because there were three of them. For the last eleven years, it had only been Jonah and her. No matter how badly he wanted to visit his friends, he had always stayed to decorate the tree with her. She loved him so dearly for that. It had been *their* family tradition.

Jonah was always helpful. She felt so guilty for monopolizing his time around Christmas but there was no one else she could ask to help her. No one else had as much passion as she did for the season. It was all about giving to others, even if it was just one day of happiness.

Sometimes he would grumble, but he would get over it when he was reminded of why he was doing it. He had such a good heart.

"What do you think, Sis? Does it pass inspection?"

She walked over and put her arm around his waist. Automatically his arm closed around her shoulder and pulled her close. She looked up at him with tears swimming in her eyes. She nodded her head.

"Oh, come on, Tauri, no tears. We have company," Jonah chided and turned to Eli.

"Christmas was our mom's favorite holiday and my dad's least favorite. She would start decorating on 'Black Friday.' My dad would always try to get her to join the other shoppers or use some other excuse to distract her. Every year he would think of something new. Nothing ever worked."

Jonah laughed, as Tauri wiped away her tears and smiled. Jonah continued his story; "eventually, dad would give in.

Even though my mom would decorate, dad would be the one pulling out the lights—checking them all to make sure they worked. If not, off he went to the store and dad hated going to the store. Huh, Sis?"

Tauri smiled as she remembered, and she wiped more tears with her free hand.

"When we were younger, he would always drop us at the mall or grocery store, give us a couple of hours, and be outside waiting when we were done."

"You two miss them a lot," in more of a statement than a question.

Jonah looked at the tree and squeezed Tauri's shoulder and said, "There're no words to say how much."

Jonah cleared his throat, kissed Tauri's hair then released her.

"I had better get going. You want to go hang out with me for a while Eli?"

"No, I'm not as young as I used to be." He looked at his watch. "It's almost 10 o'clock in Chicago—close to my bedtime."

"You're in Cali now, man. When in Rome..."

"My mind might know that, but my body hasn't caught up yet. I think I'll rest up for tree trimming tomorrow since I had a test run tonight."

"You did a good job," Tauri told him, still standing next to Jonah.

"Thank you," Eli said.

"See you later, Sis. Don't wait up."

"I don't care how late you come in Jonah. Breakfast is at nine and we will leave at ten-thirty."

"Don't worry, I'll be here," he told her, and bumped fists with Eli. "Later, man."

When the door closed behind Jonah, Tauri asked Eli, "Would you like dessert and a cup of coffee?"

"No coffee, but I will take dessert. What are we having?"

"Sweet potato pie," she said, and paused on her way to the kitchen, thinking to ask, "you do like sweet potato pie, don't you?"

"Yes," Eli answered as his eyes roamed her body.

She tried to sound normal when she asked, "are you telling me the truth, Eli? I don't like people messing over my pie. Some people think it's a little spicy."

Eli held up his right hand with a serious expression on his face.

"Honest. I would eat it with every meal if someone cooked one for me. And the spicier the better."

"Different people have different recipes. You might not like mine."

"Let me be the judge of that."

She turned and quickly walked to the kitchen. The way Eli looked at her took her breath away. By the time she reached the kitchen, her heart was beating so fast she had to sit down. *'This was all Jonah's fault.'* She exhaled. *'No, this was my fault.'* She should not have let Eli kiss her when she was in Chicago, then again right there at her own sink. But hadn't she also kissed him back in Chicago?

Tauri closed her eyes. She had to be honest with herself. She had not done anything to stop Eli from kissing her. He had even asked her for permission the last time. She warmed at the memory of their last real kiss. She had to admit Eli knew his way around a woman's mouth. And, heaven help her--she liked it. Deep down, she wished he would do it again. She could not believe he counted their kisses.

Minutes later, Tauri re-entered the living room with two pieces of pie, two forks and a can of whipped cream tucked under one arm. Eli was surprised by her mood change. He thought she would be more nervous now that they were alone. But she looked as if she had relaxed a little.

He stepped towards her before she could place the plates on the coffee table. She raised an eyebrow, but she did not step back. He picked up a fork, scooped up a heaping portion of pie and slowly put it in his mouth. He closed his eyes savoring the taste.

"Eli?"

He opened his eyes and held out a palm. She looked at him, unbelieving.

"I know you didn't just tell me to be quiet."

He swallowed.

"Yes, I did. I wasn't done."

He finished off his slice of pie in a few bites—without sitting down. Tauri stared at him in disbelief.

"Now are you done? I can't believe you just ate the pie and didn't say anything."

He stared back at her.

"Are you going to eat that piece?"

"It was my intention, but you can have it if you like."

He took the dish from her.

"Yes, I would like."

He stood in front of her as he ate—their bodies so close she could feel the heat radiating off him.

She smiled.

"You really do like it don't you?"

He nodded as he scooped another fork full of pie in his mouth. "You know, you can sit down to eat."

He shook his head.

"I like it right here," he said, as he reached for another bite.

When he'd finished the second slice, he bent down and lightly touched her lips with his.

When she only stared at him, Eli stated apologetically, "oh, I'm sorry. May I?"

Tauri was taken aback for a moment. She realized her body had been waiting for this kiss. Maybe she had been waiting for it since she left him in Chicago. What was she thinking? She could not let this happen no matter how much she had dreamed of it happening. Eli would only be here for the holidays. Then where would she be alone and missing him, but for some reason she nodded instead.

Eli's lips hovered just above hers, he shook his head, saying, "no, Tauri. I need to hear you say it."

It was just a whisper; "yes."

Eli thought he heard a little desperation there. *'That's a good sign.'* Without touching her anywhere else, he leaned in and took possession of her mouth. That was the only word his brain allowed him to come up with—possession. He leaned in further and wanted to touch her—needed to touch her—needed to hold her. But not yet.

Eli straightened as Tauri's eyes floated open. He saw the longing in her eyes. And then it was gone. He took the empty pie plate from her then placed both dishes and forks on the coffee table. He then turned back to her and removed the forgotten can of whip cream from under her arm and placed it next to the empty dishes.

"Now, where was I?" he said when he faced her again.

He wrapped his arms around her and pulled her slowly to him. The look in her brown eyes fueled his own need. His mouth swooped down on her hard and possessive. Yes, that was the right word.

Tauri trembled then moaned, opened for him and he took full advantage. She was not as relaxed as she seemed. For some reason that made him feel he had made the right decision to come to California. He poured everything he could into the kiss to convey what he was now feeling—what he had been feeling since he had first kissed her in Chicago. He tightened his hold on her and Tauri's put her arms around his shoulders.

She must have been out of her mind to let him kiss her like that. Senseless. Senseless, because she could not think of anything except how good it felt to be in his arms and how he tasted like her sweet potato pie. And those arms. Oh, those hands. Those big strong hands were roaming all over her body. Lord, she loved it, *but*. There was that 'but' again.

When he finally let her up for air she tried to speak, but...*'ohhhh;'* those lips of his were planting small kisses along her jaw line then his teeth were nibbling her ear.

"Eli," she breathed.

"Humm?"

"We shouldn't."

"Why not? You like it. I can tell."

His teeth grabbed at her bottom lip then he caught both lips up in another deep and thorough kiss. One of his hands caressed the back of her neck then stopped and held it in place as he chased her tongue with his. Man, she felt so good. He took his other hand and placed it on her behind and pulled in, to let her see just how good she felt to him.

When he broke the connection, Tauri breathed his name again, "Eli."

He lightly kissed her lips.

"You're still talking?"

She blinked then blinked again.

"It won't work, Eli."

He relaxed his hold on her but did not let her go. She repeated herself as if to make it stick this time. Her breathing labored.

"It's not going to work. You live halfway across the country. When will we ever see each other?"

"If you want something bad enough, you'll figure out a way to make it work."

She stared at him. Did she want a relationship with him that bad—bad enough to make it work? Or was she setting them both up for heartbreak.

"Eli I couldn't..."

"You couldn't or you won't?"

Those dark eyes of his seemed to look deep into her soul. Searching.

"Tauri, every man isn't like that bastard Oliver..."

"Oscar."

"Whatever. His name's not worth remembering. He left you when you needed him."

"Eli, some people can't stand to see someone they care about suffer."

"Did *he* tell you that?"

"No but..."

"Don't make excuses for him, sweetheart. He left you when you were the most vulnerable and your still worried that if you give your heart to someone else, it'll happen again."

She lowered her eyes, knowing he was partially right. She could not deny she was scared.

"Can you blame me Eli?"

"Tauri look at me."

When she would not, he gently put his finger beneath her chin and lifted it so he could see her eyes. When he had her full attention, he asked.

"Are you afraid of me?"

Her eyes widened.

"Of course not."

He smiled.

"Good."

He leaned in and kissed her softly on the lips.

"Do you believe I would hurt you?"

"Maybe not intentionally, but you'll probably get tired of not being the center of my attention."

"Tauri, you don't know that. We don't know each other well enough to know what will happen."

He stood silent for a some time, studying her face before asking, "have you dated other guys since Oscar?"

"Yes. Only two, but they didn't last past the second date."

He smiled again and traced the curve of her top lip with his thumb.

"Why are you so worried about what you think I will do in the future when no one really knows. You should be worried about what I'm doing right now."

She trembled as his tongue replaced his thumb on her lip.

"What do you mean?"

"This."

He pressed his lips to hers with a need that needed no explanation. This man was working his way into her life. This was a new feeling for her. Even with Oscar, she had not given him all of her. Letting herself go with Eli, seemed like it would be easy. He was kind, gentle when he wanted to be; considerate and patient. Her heart just would not let it happen, and she was going to tell him just as soon he finished kissing her.

Eli knew Tauri was torn. Her head was probably saying she could not make this mistake again. Her body, on the other hand, was sending him a message he could not possibly misunderstand. Why was she fighting it? This woman was driving him crazy. He had to pull up for air or they were going to go to a place that neither of them was ready to go—right here in front of the Christmas tree.

He stopped kissing her and opened his eyes. Slowly, she opened hers. His own eyes probably held the same haze.

"I think I should turn in."

The disappointment on her face gave him small thrill of satisfaction that she felt something for him.

"I won't push you, Tauri, but I want you to remember something tonight when you go to bed."

"What's that?" she asked, with frustration evident in her voice.

He reluctantly dropped his hands and stepped back.

"I want you to remember how you feel right now— physically. I want you to remember how it felt being in my arms and I want you to remember what it was like before I arrived. Compare the two and let me know which one you prefer."

Then he turned and walked away.

After she had cleaned the few dishes from their dessert and put away the remaining pie, Tauri had switched off the Christmas tree lights and went upstairs to bed. She sighed as she walked into her bathroom then turned on the shower.

Tauri *did* remember her feelings after leaving Chicago as she lay in bed trying to close her eyes. She was not as tired as she was excited. Her body felt alive again. For a few minutes, she had gotten lost in letting herself feel what Eli was doing to her. He didn't have to remind her how she had felt in his arms. How could she ever forget? It was comfortable, and exciting, and scary.

Her senses were on high alert. The taste of his mouth and the smell of his scent lingered. She could not compare Eli to Oscar. Eli was all that Oscar was not. He was caring and compassionate, attentive, and considerate. She smiled when she remembered the look in his eyes when she did not easily comply with his wishes.

Now lying here in the dark, her body wanted more. *'More of what?'* she asked herself. *'Another broken heart?'* She was so confused where Eli was concerned. Tauri willed herself to put Eli out of her mind and go to sleep. Before drifting off to sleep, the last thought was Aly's comment, *'Let it happen.'*

Chapter 13

That night, he went straight to the shower and let the cold water run over him, to calm his body down so he could sleep. As his eyes closed after getting into bed, all he could see was the longing in her eyes as they floated open when he ended the kiss. Then it was replaced by uncertainty and doubt.

At first, he had been upset, then remembered what he had told himself when he decided to go after her. Patience was what he needed. Patience was what had worked for his father. All these years his mother had been the one who was making the ripples in his parents strained relationship, but Edward had been determined and won in the end.

Eli still remembered his mother giggling like a schoolgirl as she and his dad were making out on the kitchen floor. He did not want to imagine what would have happened if he had gotten there any later.

The next morning, Eli came downstairs at eight-fifty. He was sure the warning Tauri issued to Jonah last night also extended to *him*; "breakfast is at nine—sharp."

The smell of bacon invaded his nostrils. He also smelled biscuits. And there was something else he could not quite identify. He entered the fragrant kitchen with a cheery "good morning, Tauri."

Tauri had just taken the biscuits out of the oven and placed them on the stove top. Why did the sound of his voice send shivers down her spine? *'Breathe, girl.'* She smiled, then turned to greet Eli.

"Good morning Eli. Did you sleep well?"

Eli walked over and stood much too close to her.

"Yes, I did when I finally closed my eyes. Do you know why I couldn't go to sleep right away, Tauri?"

"No, Eli. Why couldn't you sleep?"

"Because I kept tasting and smelling you," he whispered.

Tauri gasped, "Eli!"

"What's for breakfast? I'm famished!" Jonah announced as he bounced down the stairs.

Eli smiled down at Tauri then turned to greet Jonah.

"Man, you're always hungry."

"I'm a growing boy."

When Tauri gave Jonah an incredulous look, he changed his tune.

"Okay. I need energy for today."

"That's true at least. Now make yourself useful and set the table."

"Yes ma'am."

As Tauri placed the food items in the various platters and bowls, Eli carried them to the table.

"That was it," he said as he picked up a tray of mini quiches. "I couldn't identify one of the smells when I came down."

"Oh man! They will melt in your mouth." Jonah said.

When the table was set and the food all placed in the center, they all sat down. Tauri asked Jonah to say the prayer then went over the plans for the day.

Eli was amazed at the breakfast she had prepared for them. Scrambled eggs, homemade biscuits, mini quiches, breakfast potatoes, bacon, breakfast sausages and cut up fruit.

Tauri had a clipboard and was making notes as she speared a breakfast sausage with her fork.

"Okay, our schedule for today is as follows. We'll go to the senior center first and decorate their tree. By the time we arrive, their morning activities should all be completed. Jonah, I purchased some new decorations for the center, and they are in the trunk of my car."

"Tauri, you're not going to be able to see the tree because of all of the decorations," Jonah pointed out.

She made a face and told him "It's not that bad. I just get carried away sometimes. We don't have to use some of the old ones."

"Not that bad, really?" Jonah said and turned to Eli.

"Eli, Tauri is a habitual shopper. I often think the Six Days of Christmas is just a cover."

Eli asked, "How did it all start, Tauri?"

She looked at Eli.

"It's hard to explain. Cancer is a game changer. When I was first diagnosed, I zoned out for an entire three hours before I said anything to anyone. My doctor had wanted me to call someone to drive me home. Surreal was the only word I could think of at the time. I examined my life up to that point and then thought of what it might be like from that point forward. I knew then, that if God brought me through, I would make the best of the rest of my life and give back."

A silent tear slipped from her eye which she quickly wiped away.

"When I was taking my radiation and chemo treatments, the children at the center wrote me cards and drew pictures everyday of flowers, suns, happy and happy faces." She smiled then continued. "There was an endless flow of people from our church checking on me—taking me to my appointments and treatments."

"Most of the ladies from the center spent the night with me whenever I had a really bad reaction to the treatments. I have so much to be grateful for and the gift of giving is the only way of showing my appreciation."

Jonah said quietly, all teasing aside, "they don't want anything in return, Taur. They all love you very much."

"I know Jonah. But..." she paused searching for the words.

They were all quiet for a moment. Tauri cleared her throat.

"Besides, I love it and people need someone to care that they are alive—from the small child to the elderly. We all need love."

They arrived at the senior center just after the morning exercises. As Jonah had predicted, some of the ladies had invited a few of their female family members to help.

Tauri greeted the ladies as Eli and Jonah carried in the twelve-foot ladder. Next, they bought in the lights then expertly wrapped them around the tree. Eli had no doubt that Tauri had already checked each light to make sure they all were in working order.

Each of the ladies chose an ornament to place on the tree. Most of the younger women asked Jonah to place the ornaments they had chosen on the branches near the top of the tree.

Eli noticed two of the women were walking towards him with their ornaments in hand, then out of nowhere, Tauri was right in front of him with two ornaments in each hand.

"This is going well, don't you think?" she said, with a huge smile on her face.

He looked down at her and smiled.

"Yes. We have a lot of help."

He took the two items from her hands.

"We should be done in no time."

Her smile grew larger.

"Yes, we should."

The two women changed directions and turned their attention to Jonah.

"Where do you want these?" He asked.

"There," she pointed, "in that empty space near the red and brown camel."

Eli followed her directions and did as she asked. Then he turned and motioned for the remaining ornaments. He raised his brow at the other young woman.

"Over to the left of the chocolate Santa," she instructed.

"Is that it?"

"I think so."

Tauri walked over to stand beside Miss Mamie. They both looked at the gaily decorated tree.

"It looks great, doesn't it?" Tauri offered.

"Yes. Everyone did a great job," Mamie replied. "This time of year is so magical. People seem to care about each other more."

"Even if it last only a few days," Tauri said with a smile.

"Anything is better than nothing. People are generously responding and helping the less fortunate."

Tauri turned her full attention toward Miss Mamie in agreement, "Yes, there seems to be many more helping and caring for others. I believe it is because the media has made the homeless and less-fortunate more visible. Some of them may even be their neighbors."

Tauri sighed, "unfortunately, you're right. We better get going before the kid's wakeup from their naps."

Miss Mamie hugged her then held her for a moment.

"You're not pushing yourself to hard are you, honey?"

"No, Miss Mamie. I am doing just fine. The doctor gave me a clean bill of health. Besides, Claire has taken over most of my responsibilities at the centers, so I'm able to concentrate on Christmas," she said and kissed Miss Mamie on the cheek. "We'll see you tomorrow morning."

"Okay, sweetie."

Mamie released Tauri and watched her walk over to gather Jonah and Eli. Doris walked up next to her.

"Did you see that interference?"

Miss Mamie knew Doris was referring to Tauri intercepting the two young ladies before they asked Eli to place their ornaments on the tree.

"Yes. And Elijah saw it too."

Doris smiled.

"Do you think she realized how automatically she moved?"

"I don't know. But I have a feeling young Elijah is going to enlighten her."

Doris chuckled as the trio waved goodbye to everyone. "I would love to be in the room when she realizes she's in love with him."

The teachers at the daycare centers greeted Tauri warmly and quietly, as not to alert the children she was in the building. They decorated each tree and were out before the children awaken from their mid-day naps. As they said their goodbyes, Tauri invited each teacher who had volunteered to wrap toys to visit her home later that evening.

"Now see, Sis, this is what I'm talking about. It is three o'clock in the afternoon and were done already," Jonah said, as he backed out of the northern center parking space.

Tauri smiled from the back seat.

"Yep. I can get an early start on my wrapping party."

"Eli, we have to find something to do tonight," Jonah said.

"I'm up for that if Tauri doesn't need any help."

He turned in the front passenger seat to look back at her.

Tauri was momentarily stunned. At this point, she thought Eli would be ready to leave but he looked as though he was enjoying himself.

He was right, she did *not* know him. He was like no one she had ever dated. Her eyes widened. *'Did I say dating?'* What made her think of that? He was here at Jonah's request to help him for the holidays. She had to get a hold of herself.

"Tauri? Tauri, are you okay?"

She blinked and finally answered, "yes, I'm sorry. We'll be fine. You two go and enjoy yourselves. I'll save some of the refreshments for you."

Eli turned to Jonah, "I'm all yours, man."

Two hours later, Tauri placed the final touches on the table set for eight, in what she called her *wrapping room*, when the doorbell rang.

For the last two years she had prepared a light dinner for the volunteer gift wrappers. Some of the ladies came straight from work and she was so thankful they took time to help with her project.

"Coming," she called out as she hurried to the door.

LaShelle was the first to arrive.

"LaShelle! You're early!" Tauri said with a big smile then pulled her into a big hug.

"Hello Miss Tauri. I hope you don't mind," LaShelle said shyly.

"It's Tauri. And of course not."

When Tauri opened the first center she had instructed her teachers and the rest of her staff to address any adult by either Mr. or Miss in the presence of the children.

"Come in! I just finished setting the table."

LaShelle inhaled and said, "it smells good in here."

"Thank you. It's the bayberry and cranberry candles. I love the smells of Christmas."

They walked into the wrapping room.

"Have a seat. Would you like something to drink?"

LaShelle sat.

"No thank you. Not yet."

Tauri looked at the wall clock.

"It's still a little early. Is everything alright?",

"I saw Jonah yesterday."

"I was wondering if he saw you. He didn't comment on it."

LaShelle bowed her head.

"He wouldn't look at me Tauri. All I wanted was to tell him what happened before he left for Chicago, and the reason I couldn't go with him."

Tears fell onto LaShelle's hands, folded in her lap.

Tauri grabbed a napkin from the table and handed it to her. She touched LaShelle's knee as she wiped her tears and looked up.

"I know it's been a long time, but I think he's been running away from it," Tauri said. "Let him think about it for a while longer. Our parents taught him better than that. If I know him, and I do, he will apologize because it will bother him until he does."

"Miss Tauri...Tauri, please don't say anything to him about this."

"No worries. I've learned to stay out of Jonah's personal life. I'll keep my distance unless you ask me to say something." The doorbell rang again.

"Are you okay?"

LaShelle sniffed and nodded.

"Go fix your face. And don't forget, I'm here if you need someone to talk to."

Tauri watched LaShelle walk to the bathroom down the hallway then sighed. She knew her brother did not forgive easily but she hoped this case would be an exception. She walked over to the door and opened it to her wrapping party guests.

"Hello ladies!"

Eli sat in the passenger seat as Jonah drove them to a meeting with some of his friends from high school. Eli chose to wear a pair of gray slacks with a deep purple, long sleeved, open necked shirt and a jacket. Jonah had dressed in a similar fashion with black slacks, and a deep pink shirt with a light jacket.

Eli looked at Jonah's profile as the vehicle stopped at a red light.

"You've been pretty quiet today."

"Yeah, Sorry. I'm not being a good host; am I?"

"I just noticed since yesterday, after we put the tree up at the center and this afternoon, you kept looking at the doorway."

"Was I that obvious?"

"I don't think your sister noticed. She was pretty busy."

Jonah glanced at Eli.

"Oh believe me, if you noticed, so did Tauri. LaShelle and I have history together. She was the 'One.' *The One.* Is there really a "One"?"

Eli didn't answer. Jonah continued.

"We met on a blind date, although at the time I didn't know it. My friends told me it was just a small gathering," Jonah laughed, "but everyone was paired up except…"

"You and LaShelle," Eli interjected.

"Yes. Some of our mutual friends thought it would be good if we got to know each other. At least Tauri hasn't tried that one on me yet. Anyway, we hit it off. I found out she was from the neighborhood not too far from where we lived. Her mom raised her alone after her dad was killed in a convenience store robbery. He was driving the getaway car."

"Damn!"

"Yeah!"

"She told you that on the first day?"

"No. It took a few months for her to open up. She would come by the sandwich shop after school since she went to school across town. I asked her why she went to a school so far from her home and she told me it was because of her dad. The store was near her home, so when she arrived at school the next day the kids were all talking about it.

"Her mom used her sister's address and switched her school. She was *so* very book smart and helped me with my homework many times. But all that changed when I went to Stanford… we only saw each other during school breaks.""

"Why didn't she go with you to Chicago?"

"She said she didn't want to leave her mother."

He turned the vehicle right at the light then right again into a restaurant parking lot and parked. Then he faced Eli. "After I returned home from my second interview with you. I tried to talk her into coming with me and we could make room for her mother…" Jonah sighed. "LaShelle said she'd found another boyfriend and it was over between us."

"That's rough."

"Yeah. You know what they say—it is what it is. I hope you like seafood."

Eli thought he knew Jonah fairly well. But sometimes you never know a person as well as you think you do.

After finishing their dinner, Jonah took Eli to the game room in the back of the restaurant. Jonah introduced him to a dozen of his male friends ranging from Jonah's age to seventy-five years old. Some played Poker, others played Dominos and Bid Whist.

Eli laughed at the jokes and listened attentively to the wisdom of the older men. Jonah told him he had grown up in these rooms. He had come here when Tauri was too motherly, or to give her a break. She was aware of the game room and had approved understanding they were a community that looked after their own.

When Jonah and Eli arrived at the house, Tauri had gone to bed and had left them a snack in the fridge.

Chapter 14

The following morning at breakfast, Tauri recapped the duties she'd already assigned to Jonah. She tasked Eli to manage the clean-up crew. She informed him he was going to be on his feet all day and watched him closely for his reaction. He'd told her that he was up for it.

Jonah maneuvered Tauri's pick up around to the back of the building—to the alternate parking lot. Whatever Eli expected when they arrived at the location of Tauri's next project, this was not it. Hundreds of people were already lined up, waiting for a hot meal and maybe some companionship.

"Wow," Eli muttered.

"Yes," Tauri said with a sigh, from the back seat. "The poor economy has forced a lot more families onto the streets. Others are spending their entire paycheck keeping a roof over their heads."

"I can't tell you how many parents wanted to pull their children out of daycare because either the dad or the mom had been laid off."

"I thought the economy was doing well," Eli commented.

"The *economy is* doing well. They are building more and more housing but most of the citizens can't afford them."

"Believe it or not," Jonah added. "The new housing prices push the surrounding rents up so the people who already live there can no longer afford them," Jonah said as he parked and turned off the engine.

They all climbed out and went in through the back entrance. The large warehouse-like room was filled with long tables covered with white plastic tablecloths. The tables, at least thirty, were formed in a U-shape. All the chairs were placed around the outside with teams of young people placing plastic knives, spoons and forks wrapped in napkins at each place setting.

As they walked, Jonah accepted hugs and chatted with old acquaintances. Tauri introduced Eli as a friend of Jonah's from Chicago. He would have to discuss that with her later. Eli followed Tauri to the kitchen area located in the left corner of the large room, where he asked, "How many volunteers are involved in this project?"

"Oh, about a hundred or so. Only the group leaders attended the meetings but at last count, it was reported we would have close to one hundred and fifty both on and off site. A portion of them work behind the scenes. Some were here this morning, before sunup, to set up tables and make sure everything was clean. Others donated or cooked the food. Most everyone here has been participating in this event since its inception ten years ago."

She motioned toward a group of teenage boys.

"You'll be in charge of those young men. There are about twenty of them. They'll make sure the trash is emptied, help lift any heavy items, and act as a fill ins."

When Eli frowned, Tauri added, "whenever anyone needs a break, someone from your team will fill in. They will also need to help with teardown and cleanup. A few of the local high schools offered to give the students extra credit if they worked here today. They know you'll have to sign their slips when the day is done, so I don't think you'll have any problems."

Eli was so in awe of this woman with the big brown eyes. Just outside the kitchen, a serving line was set up with burners already flaming, awaiting the chafing dishes. To his right, cakes and other desserts were being placed on small paper plates. Next to that, a table held paper cups and punch.

When they stepped through the kitchen door, Eli was amazed at the activity. The dozen or so people wearing plastic caps, aprons and gloves were busy ladling hot food into chafing dishes. Eli saw pots of greens, and platers of turkey (whole and cutup) chicken, ham, potato salad, dressing, yams, green beans and cornbread. He was surprised Tauri had not volunteered to bring anything with her this morning.

"Tauri?"

Eli looked over in time to notice some familiar faces from the senior center. Tauri saw Miss Mamie, flashed a brilliant, heartfelt smile and walked into Miss Mamie's outstretched arms. They kissed each other on the cheek and stayed in each other's embrace.

Eli smiled and thought, they just saw each other yesterday.

"How are you, baby?" Miss Mamie asked her.

"Fine, Miss Mamie. How are you?"

Tauri pulled back from the embrace but did not completely let go.

"I'm fine, child. I'm old. I'm gonna have some aches and pains now and then."

Tauri studied the elderly woman's face carefully, then frowned and asked, "did you do any of this cooking?"

"All I cooked was a turkey."

Tauri stared at Miss Mamie.

"Miss Mamie, and?"

Eli noticed she used the same tone with the older woman that she did with Jonah when he was irritating her. *Does this woman mother everyone?'*

Miss Mamie lifted her chin, and admitted, "and a peach cobbler."

"Miss Mamie, you know better than to push yourself so hard this time of year."

"It's not so much, baby. My daughter and granddaughter will be cooking Christmas dinner: so I thought, why not? And you know I couldn't miss today. Besides, I'm fine."

Tauri didn't seem convinced.

"You *do* look a little tired to me. Promise me you'll take it easy today. Let all of us take care of things," she said stepping back from Miss Mamie's embrace and turning to Eli. "Jonah and I brought extra help."

"Elijah," Miss Mamie said with a smile and outstretched her arms again.

Eli walked over and bent down to hug and kiss her.

"Good to see you again," Miss Mamie said. "You decided to hang around after the last few days?"

"Yes, ma'am. Tauri's been taking it easy on me," Eli said and turned to smile at Tauri.

Tauri felt heat rise up her neck as the two of them gazed at her. Eli was making her feel things she did not want to feel. He was so easy and comfortable around her friends and family— like he was the missing piece of her life.

Jonah came into the kitchen as the last of the filled chafing dishes were carried to their places.

"Morning, everyone!"

The hellos and greetings were called out. He grinned and hugged and kissed Miss Mamie and said, "Hi Beautiful."

The older woman blushed. Jonah winked at her and announced as he walked out the door, "It's show time everyone!"

Eli smiled at both women and followed Jonah out the door, saying, "I guess I'd better gather my crew."

Tauri frowned as she watched Miss Mamie smile at Eli's retreating back. She decided to let it go for now. Like Jonah said, it was show time.

She walked out and noticed Eli surrounded by teenaged boys, each one paying close attention to what he was saying. Tauri walked over and stood in the U of tables and greeted the guests as they were directed to their seats. Within minutes, the chairs were all filled.

Servers, who were mostly teenaged girls, were dispatched to the tables with hot plates of food and drinks. Tauri saw Eli walk into the kitchen. When he returned, he had at least a dozen serving trays. She watched as he gave one to each of the teenage boys and they walked over to the serving line. He paired the servers with his guys.

As the young man held the tray, the server loaded at least a half dozen plates on the first tray. Then they both went back to the tables. Then the next server started to load her tray.

Tauri was beyond impressed. Eli had probably cut down their serving time by half. Jonah came over and nudged her as they watch Eli directing both the servers and tray carriers.

"Not bad, huh?" Jonah prompted.

Tauri had to smile.

"Yeah, not bad. The day is still young."

Jonah smiled, shook his head, and walked away.

The day went like clockwork. As soon as a group or a person was finished and asked if they wanted seconds, the vacated space was cleaned and set up for the next person. Each one of the guests had been given a ticket when they walked in, to receive their pick of free apparel, shoes, purses, hygiene kits, gifts for kids and blankets.

Halfway through the day, Eli was given a plate of food. He ate standing in the corner, keeping an eye on his crew, making sure they took breaks. He also made sure the ones who were not carrying a tray, were emptying the trash.

On occasion he would search out Tauri. He watched as she knelt and talked to a couple of kids, hugged a crying mother and shared a laugh with one of the older gentlemen. By the expression on her face after she had finished talking to one young mother he knew her heart had gone out to her. Their eyes met across the room. He could not tell from so far away, but he was sure there were unshed tears in her eyes.

By the end of the day, Eli was so tired he just wanted to fall over on anything that would hold him. As soon as the last person exited the room, he dispatched his crew of young people to fold up the tables as soon as they were cleaned. Within the hour, all tables and chairs were folded. Some were stacked in a back-storage room and the borrowed ones were loaded into a large trailer.

Eli looked across the room at a teenaged boy by the name of Taylor, if he remembered right. He was slowly pushing a broom across the floor as three teenaged girls flanked him and talked as they walked. One of the young ladies was carrying a large dustpan. *'Oh, to be young again,'* he thought.

Jonah came over and stood next to Eli.

"Man, I'm tired!" Jonah exclaimed.

Eli frowned as he looked at the younger man because he looked as energetic as he did when he came in.

Eli smiled faintly, and answered, "Most definitely. Tired enough for three people, but it's the best tired I've ever felt."

He eyed Jonah. "You don't *look* tired and I know I saw you buzzing around here as much as Tauri and I were."

Jonah smiled, "Oh I'm too used to it. I know what to expect."

Then he looked around the large empty room.

"Before we got involved with this ministry, Tauri and I delivered food along with our church to home bound seniors and shut ins. When Tauri became so busy with her daycare centers, she signed all those needy folks up with a state-run program offering the same services, more frequently.

"We would also go out looking for people—especially children, in the places known to be used by the homeless. Tauri would volunteer her center to keep the preschool children for the day while the parents looked for work. *Or*, she would help them find assistance. The state made it a priority to help parents with children find shelter. She even tried to bring home a family once."

Jonah waved his hand around, saying, "believe me this is *so* much better. I shudder to think about Tauri still going to some of the places we'd ventured to alone, to take food or clothing to the homeless."

They were both quiet for a moment. Eli did not want to think of Tauri doing that either. Jonah put a hand on Eli's shoulder and grinned at him.

"Don't worry. This was the toughest day of the whole week. Tomorrow, we have two parties and then Christmas at the beach."

The three of them walked into the foyer, at the house, at seven-forty-seven. Jonah looked at Tauri and Eli and shook his head.

"You two look like you are going to drop where you are standing."

"I almost feel like it," Tauri said.

She frowned at him.

"You don't look like you've spent all day on your feet."

"Hey! That's because of my elf trainee here."

He pointed to Eli.

"My job was easy this year."

"I guess. Well, I'm going to take a shower before I fix us a light dinner."

"Nothing for me, Sis. I promised Deja we'd go out to dinner."

"Alright. She didn't make it to the wrapping party. Tell her I said hi. And I'll see her tomorrow."

"Okay. I'm going to hit the shower then I'm out." Jonah said, as he headed for the stairs.

"How does he do it?" Eli asked as he stared at Jonah bounding up the stairs.

Tauri smiled. "He grumbles about my list every year, but I think he gets as much enjoyment as I do when he helps someone else."

Eli nodded and commented, "I'm going to take a shower also and I'll be back down. This morning I noticed there were still a few sandwiches left from last night."

As Eli took his hot shower, he thought about the events of the day. Every one of the volunteers worked hard to make a great day for people less fortunate than themselves.

He was pleasantly surprised by the teenagers. Their nationalities were across the board but the majority of them were African American. Not all teenagers were hanging out in the streets or caring about themselves. He'd had conversations with some of the young men while they were waiting for the first wave of people to finish their meals. He found that over half of them were college bound at the end of the school year. The others had a few years to go but they all seemed to be a good group of kids. They all were from different backgrounds, yet they got along well.

Eli finished his shower and changed into a pair of loose-fitting sweatpants and a short-sleeved t-shirt that read 'Chicago, The Windy City.' He yawned as he ambled down the stairs. He heard the front door close and knew it was Jonah leaving for his dinner date with Deja.

Tauri was already in the kitchen placing sandwiches on a decorative platter. She must have sensed he was in the doorway of the kitchen. She looked up and smiled.

"What would you like to drink?"

Eli returned the smile.

"Do you have any more of that strawberry lemonade?"

"Yes, and why are you grinning?"

"Those pajama's look very comfortable."

Tauri looked down at her seasonal pjs. They were light green with tiny decorated Christmas trees and tiny Santa's carrying bags of toys over their shoulders.

"Yes, they are."

She turned and took two glasses from the cabinet, opened the refrigerator, and pulled out a pitcher of freshly squeezed pink lemonade.

"Every year, for as far back as I can remember, our parents gave us a pair of pjs for Christmas. It was one of the gifts we were allowed to open on Christmas Eve," she said and paused. "Would you like ice?"

"No, thank you."

She put ice in one of the glasses from the dispenser in the fridge door and placed it on the tray.

"This was the last pair of pjs my mom bought me before she died."

"I'm sorry. I didn't mean to make you sad."

She sighed, then poured lemonade into both glasses.

"It's alright. They are good memories."

Eli nodded.

"Let me get that tray."

"Okay. I'll get the pie and I'll be right in."

When Tauri came into the living room, Eli had put the tray on the coffee table and taken a seat on the sofa. He looked like he belonged there—so relaxed in his sweatpants and short sleeved shirt. Tauri wondered what it would be like to see Eli every evening before bed. Aly's words tumbled around in her head again, *'Let it happen'*.

"Did I sit in the wrong place?"

She shook her head.

"No, you're fine."

She placed the two pieces of dessert on the table next to the tray, and asked, "would you like to watch a movie?"

Tauri walked over and flicked a switch behind the sofa and the tree lit up.

"Don't tell me," Eli teased. "Let me guess the title."

Tauri laughed out loud.

"That's not funny."

Then she laughed even harder.

Eli loved the sound of her laughter. He wished he could hear that laughter every day for the rest of his life. When she stood next to him, he pulled her onto his lap. His head swooped down and captured her lips so quickly, it surprised him. Greedily, he kissed her mouth wanting to taste her. He wanted to draw her into the way he was feeling.

She opened her mouth to him quickly and urgently. His hands were all over her body and her hands were as busy as his. What was this woman doing to him? It was like he was under a spell and he was going willingly.

When she moaned, he pulled back for some much-needed air. He frowned at her.

"Tauri, you must know you're like a drug to me. I can't take my eyes off of you. When I was away from you this week, I wondered what you were doing. I couldn't wait to get back to you."

"Eli," she whispered.

Eli didn't let her finish.

"Tauri, I want to make love to you so bad my teeth hurt,"

Tauri's eyes grew big then she started to laugh again.

"I didn't know I was such a comedian."

"Eli," she said touching his face. "It's not you, but you do make me laugh."

She sat beside him on the sofa.

"I don't sleep around Eli. I still have some thinking to do about us."

"So, there is an 'Us'?" Eli asked. "I don't know you that well, but I was hopeful there would be an 'us.'"

"I'm still thinking about that, too. I don't want to get either of our hopes up by sleeping with you. It would not just be sex to me. My entire being would be attached to the meaning behind it. Do you understand what I'm saying?"

"I do. More than you know. I don't sleep around either, Tauri. When Phyllis told me in so many words that I was a fool to go out to start my own business, I was devastated. I have always been careful how I love and who I love. We had been dating for three years and we had been intimate for two of them.

"I thought she was my life partner until she showed me who she really was and what she really wanted. Since then, all my energy has been funneled into getting the business started.""

"What business?" Tauri asked.

Eli cleared his throat and looked away from Tauri, to the food on the coffee table. Only his family and his boss knew of his plans to start his own business. After Phyllis, Eli had been very careful who he told about his dream.

"Are you sure you want to hear about it?"

"Eli, I'm sure you know, I am aware of how exciting it is to finally get to the point where you say, 'okay, it's time.' I was fortunate when I thought I was ready to open the first daycare center. I had support from everyone I spoke to about it. The first person I spoke to was Miss Mamie. She told me a hard truth. Everyone around you isn't going to be happy for or supportive of you. More importantly, don't let anyone talk you out of your dream."

"Miss Mamie is a wise woman."

"I know. She says it comes with living."

Tauri reached for his hand.

"Let's pray first and then you can tell me all about it while we eat."

As they ate, Eli told her about the people he worked with and for.

"We have three teams in the agency, each targeting a specific demographic. My secretary, Iris, talks to all of the applicants, then sends them to the group she thinks would benefit from their background and creativity."

"I talk to her all the time," Tauri said, raising a brow. "I speak to her whenever Jonah doesn't answer his phone."

"She's that good?" Tauri asked.

"She's been in the business for over twenty-five years. I remember when she told me I needed to interview Jonah. I asked him what he'd do for a new client we had just acquired. His inputs were very impressive. Fresh out of college and he had his finger on the pulse of advertising to young America."

Tauri smiled.

"He *was* in the top five percent of his class."

"Yes, I know, Miss Proud Sister." "Can you blame me? He had a very difficult time after our parents passed away. I was so afraid for his future. I wanted him to go to an historically black university or college, but the only one in California is Charles R. Drew University of Medicine and Science in L.A.

Jonah didn't want to go into medicine or be too far away from *me*. So, after applying to most of the colleges with a good business program in the state, he was accepted into Stanford. We also made a deal. If he was offered a job out of state, I told him he had to take it. He had four years to think about it."

Eli handed her a fork for her pie.

"He was just worried about you."

"I know but he had his entire life in front of him and I didn't want him to lose out on the best opportunities of life, hanging around me. Isn't that what you're looking for Eli? The best opportunities in life?"

"Yes. Like me coming to California for Christmas. The opportunity to spend this week with you and Jonah. I'm not going to lie. Today was an eye opener for me."

"In what way?"

"I've never really thought about the homeless much. I would just see someone on the corner or on the sidewalk. I'd give them a few dollars, but I would keep moving. My mom volunteers for different charities, although I've never spoken with her about it. I remember she would donate mine and Sheila's old clothes when we outgrew them. I guess I never really thought about it that much."

"Well, I thank you for being honest. I was doing some research last week about the homeless in the United States. California and New York have the largest homeless population and it was said they estimate about a half a million people are homeless across the nation."

"I know we fed close to a thousand people today."

"Counting children, I think Miss Mamie said eight hundred and seventeen. Most of the people who came through today are from the local community."

Eli piggybacked her sentiment.

"I guess when you have to choose between the electricity, heat and the rent or mortgage, a special holiday dinner is not high on your list of priorities."

"Right. There are a few churches in the city that have food ministries throughout the year. I wish I could do more, especially for the children."

They were both quiet for a while. Then Tauri stood and looked down at Eli's empty pie plate.

"Would you like another slice of pie?"

He smiled up at her.

"No, thank you. It was delicious and so was the sandwich."

She smiled back.

"You're welcome. Let me put these in the dishwasher and I'll be right back. The remote is right there. The DVD should be in the player."

"Oh man, I thought you forgot."

"You've got jokes," she smirked and left the room.

Minutes later, Eli looked over as Tauri stood in the doorway in her Christmas pjs.

"I'm all done."

"Come here."

Eli held out his hand and she did not disappoint him. He pulled her down on him then gave her a quick kiss.

"Mmmm, that was good," Tauri purred.

"There's more where that came from, sweetheart. Just let me know."

She snuggled close.

"I like it when you surprise me."

"That's good to know. Are you ready for your movie?"

Tauri nodded and Eli pressed play on the remote.

"Here goes viewing number three hundred and..."

Tauri threw her head back and laughed. Eli kissed her again. It felt good to hold her in his arms. They watched the movie in silence. He looked down a few times and saw her eye lids were starting to droop.

"Are you going to sleep on me, Tauri?"

She held her head back to reveal very droopy eyes.

"No," she answered, refocussing on the television screen. "I like this part where he asked Mary what she wanted."

After a while Eli, felt her breathing change and knew she had fallen asleep. He would try and be chivalrous and carry her up to her room, but as tired as he was, they would not make it. The last thing he remembered was saying to the woman sleeping in his arms,

"I'll lasso the moon for you, Tauri."

Jonah returned early the next morning. He found the Christmas tree lights blinking in the family room and assumed Tauri must have forgotten to turn them off. This time of year, he sometimes had forgotten too.

In past years, he and Tauri would sometimes work late into the night to make sure all her projects were completed. Over the years, he had come to look forward to Tauri's "Six Days of Christmas".

Tauri had always told him they would, in whatever circumstances, give back in gratitude to their neighbors and parent's friends who had helped them after their parents had died. Everyone had been there for them both and especially when Tauri went through her bout with cancer. He shivered at the thought of those days and he was glad they were over. Tauri was forever grateful and diligent to give back wherever she saw the need.

Jonah entered the room and came to an abrupt halt. Eli was laid back on the sofa with his legs stretched out and Tauri's head lay on his chest. Eli held her securely in his arms. Jonah had wondered if something had happened between them during Tauri's visit to Chicago. Ever since her return, she had not mentioned Eli, and Eli was the same. Jonah noticed they both had been in foul moods lately. He'd played a hunch and he had been right. *'Uh huh, they do care about each other.'*

Chapter 15

Tauri opened her eyes and stared for a moment at the tree. The sun shined brightly through the window behind the gaily decorated Christmas tree, making it look as beautiful as it had been the night before. Disoriented, she breathed in Eli's scent surrounding her. The scent she had remembered from her time in Chicago where he had taken such good care of her. She had tried hard to forget it, but she could not. His wonderful act of kindness was a gift. *'Oh man, I fell asleep on him—again.'*

A bright colored throw covered them as Eli's chest moved up and down easily as he slept. There was no way she could get up without waking him. He had said yesterday how tired he had been. Tauri pushed back her hair and raised her head to look into Eli's face. Eli tightened his arms around her. She did not pretend it didn't feel good, waking up in his arms. She relaxed for a moment and let herself really feel him holding her and she wanted it—needed it.

She glanced up again. He looked so peaceful, almost as if he fell asleep on her sofa every night. What would it be like to wake up in his arms every morning—to feel cherished the way she did whenever he was around?

The moments those thoughts entered her head, Tauri pushed them away. Eli was only there until Christmas. He would tolerate busy times for now but what about later, when she worked on her annual fundraisers and not see her bed until midnight?

Someone blew a car horn outside and Eli jerked. His eyes slowly opened, and he squinted against the bright light of the sun. Instinctively, he tightened his hold around the woman who lay in his arms. Slowly, she looked up.

"Good morning, sweetheart," he said with a smile forming on his lips.

"Good morning, Eli."

He frowned at her forlorn expression.

"What's wrong?"

"You couldn't have slept very well."

"Why do you say that?"

"Your head was at an odd angle. Does your neck hurt?"

"No," he said, still looking and smiling down at her. "But I know something else that hurts."

"Oh, am I hurting you? I'm sorry, let me get up."

He shook his head when she tried to push herself up.

"Eli! You said you were hurting..."

She paused when she finally understood what he meant. Tauri's eyes widened. She pushed against his chest to release her. He held her tighter and chuckled.

"I'm just telling you the truth. What do you expect, lying on top of me like that all night?"

"Eli," she cautioned.

"What?" he said, feigning innocence.

She rolled her eyes at him. He took her chin in his hand and turned her head to look at him.

"Sweetheart, I am not going to hide, ignore, nor deny my reaction to you. I like being around you. I like talking to you. I like holding you. I like almost everything about you.

Tauri's heart began to melt a little, but only a little. This was a good way to get her heart broken. No man had ever said those things to her before. While Oscar had always told her she was beautiful, he never made her feel special and powerful. Did Eli really mean it or was he just saying it only to sleep with her?

"Eli, what do you mean by 'almost'?"

His thumb caressed her cheek.

"We've only known each other for a short while and there is a lot about each other we don't know. I would love to know all there is to know about Miss Tauri Hill."

"Miss Tauri Shamela Hill," she said with a smile playing around her mouth.

He chuckled and kissed her temple,

"Tauri Shamela Hill -- that's nice."

"Thank you."

Suddenly her eyes widened again. *'Jonah!'* She pushed against Eli's chest again, and he released her. She stood and looked at him, her brow crushed together in a fierce frown.

"What's wrong?"

"Jonah has to be home. Do you think he saw us?"

Eli didn't mention the fact they were both covered with a throw he did not remember getting.

"And what if he did?" he said, still lying back looking up at her with one of his arms under his head.

"What do you *think?*"

She looked at the Christmas tree.

"Did you turn the tree lights off during the night?"

"No."

"That means he did. Oh!"

She almost looked frantic to Eli.

"Tauri, he knows you have your own life. Why would you think anything would be wrong with the fact that we were on the sofa asleep?"

She did not look convince with her new hairdo tossed around her beautiful face, Eli wondered what would it look like after a night in bed together?

Tauri put her hands on her hips.

"Eli?"

"What?"

"Don't look at me like that."

"Like what, sweetheart?"

"Like you want to eat me for breakfast."

Heat snaked up her neck to her face as she realized the mistake in her choice of words. His smile only grew bigger.

Tauri overcame the blush with irritation. She narrowed her eyes.

"But I do, sweetheart."

Now her eyes were only slits.

"Okay. Okay," Eli capitulated. "I'll calm down, but this conversation is not over."

Tauri turned to walk away then stopped and turned to faced Eli again.

"We don't have to go out today until eleven-thirty. I'll cook something light—maybe quiche and pancakes in an hour or so."

Then she turned and walked away.

As Eli bounced up the stairs, Jonah came out of his room dressed in a black tee shirt, running shorts and tennis shoes.

"Morning!"

"Morning man. You want to go for a run?"

"You bet. Give me five."

"I'll be downstairs."

Eli went into his room and searched for the one pair of running shorts he thought to throw into his suitcase. He knew he would have to discuss what Jonah had seen when he came in this morning. Although Tauri was Jonah's older sister, he may still feel it was his duty to protect her when he thought it was warranted.

The sky was clear and blue. The air was crisp, but to Eli it felt good. During the winter months, he took his runs at the gym or on the treadmill in his spare bedroom. This was way better. A they ventured out the front door, Jonah yelled up to Tauri they were going on a run then they were on their way.

The neighborhood boasted well-manicured lawns and although it was December, some of them looked like green carpets. Some of the neighbors were already outside enjoying the beautiful morning. Three men were outside with their coffee cups, having a conversation.

"Merry Christmas, gentlemen!" Jonah called out.

"Merry Christmas Jonah!" They said in unison.

One yelled out, "say hi to Tauri!"

"Will do!" Jonah said as he threw up his hand and ran down the street.

Eli had to kick a little to keep up with the younger man. They were twenty minutes into the run before Jonah signaled for him to stop at a local park bench.

"This is a beautiful neighborhood." Eli said with labored breath.

"Yeah. Our dad grew up in the house. Almost all of our neighbors have been here just as long."

Eli thought Jonah did not sound as if they had just run a little over three miles. *'He's not even breathing hard.'*

"After our parents passed and the house become ours, we did our best to keep it in excellent shape. Even though Tauri is so very busy, she has done a great job keeping up on the maintenance."

"She looks like she does a good job on everything she tackles."

"Yeah, she's so much smarter than I am and is also so very good with people. She has never had any problem getting anyone to do anything for her."

Eli knew that to be true where he was concerned. He would do whatever she asked. But it sounded like Jonah was just making small talk. Eli was never one to beat around the bush as his Grand used to say—he wanted to get to the inevitable.

"Jonah. We need to talk about this morning."

Jonah frowned into the sun as he looked at Eli.

"Is she worried about it?"

"Freaked out is what I would say."

"She's a grown woman. She's allowed."

"But she is still your older sister and wants to look respectable in your eyes. She cares about what you think."

"I know and I want her to be happy, Eli. She's lived alone for a long time and I know she wants a family. She gave up so much when our parents died. Sometimes I regret the hard time I gave her."

"From what I know about your sister, she doesn't regret one day of it."

"Yeah, thanks Eli. I know you're right, but I still think about it sometimes."

"I don't think you have anything to worry about."

Eli did not know what he would say next because at the moment, he didn't know what his next step with Tauri might be. He was not going to push her into anything she was not comfortable with.

"Look Jonah, I don't know what is going to happen with me and Tauri. I am not going to go any faster than she wants me to. She would like to have a relationship, but she is scared because of that bastard Oliver."

"Oscar."

"Whatever. He messed her up good. If he would have stuck around, he would have known what a terrific and loving person Tauri really is."

Jonah smiled when he asked, "you're in love with her, aren't you?"

Eli sat down on the bench, then stared up at Jonah.

"I don't know."

He knew he did not feel this way about Phyllis. He had never seen her doing any charity work or care about anyone but herself. What had he ever seen in her?

"Well you don't have that long to think about it, but I have to tell you Eli, don't hurt her. She went through a lot when Oscar turned his back on her."

Jonah was right. Eli was scheduled to leave the day after Christmas. Leaving him only two days to look inside himself and to convince Tauri they could work.

"I know. I'll try not to."

On the run back to the house, Eli thought long and hard about what Jonah had asked him. Was he in love with Tauri? If he was, it felt pretty good.

He still had to talk to Jonah about becoming his partner before he went back to Chicago. When they arrived back at the house, Tauri must have heard them because she came to the door and announced brunch would be served in thirty minutes. Jonah had really kicked the last mile forcing Eli to show the young exec he was no push over.

When they both caught their breath, Jonah flipped open the top of a small box on the side of the garage door and punched in a five-digit code. The panel door activated. Eli did not realize there was a refrigerator in the corner of the garage. Jonah grabbed two bottles of water and tossed one to Eli.

"Thanks."

Eli removed the top then guzzled half before he spoke.

"Jonah, I'm leaving DHP."

Jonah was in the middle of taking a drink of water when he erupted into a fit of coughing. Eli walked over and thumped him on the back.

"You alright?"

Jonah coughed again and again before he was able to speak.

"You're what?"

"I was going to tell you when we finished with the recycling company."

"What about the team?"

"I was going to tell them after I spoke with you."

"Why?"

"Because I want you to come with me."

"Where are you going? To the competition?"

"Yes and no. It's my company and if you decide to come with me it would be our company."

Eli concentrated on Jonah's every facial expression and his body language. Jonah sighed and coughed a few more times, as he continued to drink more water. Jonah walked out of the garage and back into the morning sun. Eli spoke quickly; "it won't be easy. I already talked to DH."

"And..." Jonah asked, without turning around.

"He's not happy. I agreed not to leave until we completed this last campaign. He asked me not to take any of the agency's clients with me and I would have to find my own replacement before I go. DHP is one of the industry leaders and they will survive."

The younger man turned and faced Eli.

"What about the team and Iris?"

Eli knew what he was saying. The team was like a well-oiled instrument of DHP. DH knew whatever client or project he assigned to the team they would make them a household name.

"They will be encouraged to work with the new team leader and continue in their current capacity. Don't worry about Iris, she's planning on retiring at the end of this year."

Jonah continued to stare at him, so Eli rushed on to say, "I have a business plan all drawn up. It's been reviewed by my new brother in-law, Mitchell Brennen."

"Brennen is your brother-in-law?" Jonah asked amazed.

Mitchell Brenn's business savvy was well known. The reputation of the multi-millionaire genius preceded him. His endorsement added clout to Eli's proposal.

Eli continued; "you don't have to make up your mind now but at least tell me you'll think about it."

The two men stood and stared at each other for what seemed like forever to Eli. Finally, Jonah said, "email me the business plan, then let me talk to Tauri about it. I'll let you know after the holidays."

"Sounds good. I'll send it to as soon as I go upstairs."

Jonah nodded. They slapped hands then rushed upstairs to the showers.

As Eli showered, he contemplated his future. When Jonah asked him if he loved Tauri, he had not known what to say. The only thing he did know was when she left Chicago, his world had somehow been changed. He had not been able to concentrate on his work and had been easily irritated.

Usually he was the even-tempered, efficient person in the office. He was sure the team noticed but no one had commented on it. Even his daily routine had not been the same. Tauri Hill had invaded his life and he did not think it would ever be the same until he figured out how he felt about her.

Just the sight of her stopped him in his tracks. Her heart was kind and caring. She was funny. She was beautiful, smart and his family would love her. He knew now for sure what he wanted. He wanted her. He had probably wanted her the first time he had seen her in the grocery store.

He mentally shook himself. *'Where did that come from?'* Hadn't he come out to California to see if this is what he wanted? Since he now knew, he had to make her see they could make it work.

Before he had met Phyllis Emery, he had been in relationships with short term, temporary goals—just a little companionship for the holidays or a party date. He had not wanted anything to interfere with the starting his own advertising agency. Eli thought she would be the one. She had the classy, sophisticated, stylish looks of the woman he had always envisioned as his wife. During their three-year relationship, she had always been agreeable until he told her about his dream.

As he and Jonah continued to bring in new clients to DHP, Phyllis began to make subtle suggestions that maybe he should rethink opening his own company. She had told him to play it safe and stay with DHP because the economy was not very favorable. Eli thought she would see the potential once he organized a new team and moved successfully forward.

Phyllis had their future already mapped out. A home in the suburbs, the number of kids they would have and what schools would be best. He had always indulged her and hoped she would

would stand by him. The day he showed her the business plan and informed the owner of DHP of his intentions, Phyllis had voiced her disapproval and walked out on him without even looking back.

Half an hour later, Eli was showered and dressed in a pair of black slacks, a long-sleeved forest green pullover, and a pair of his favorite black loafers. The smell of bacon met him as he opened the bedroom door. His stomach rumbled in anticipation as he rushed downstairs.

When he reached the bottom step, he was frozen by the sight of Tauri Hill—so fresh and vibrant as she moved efficiently around the kitchen preparing brunch. Eli had pushed himself to hurry down so he could spend a few minutes with her before Jonah came down.

He was glad he had a run and a talk with Jonah after the sweet wake up he had that morning. He did not know how much more of this he could take but he would not force Tauri to make any decision or do anything she did not want to.

Eli had never been a selfish man but his dream of opening his own advertising agency was so deep in his blood, it had become part of him. As he watched Tauri remove a pan of what looked like croissants from the oven, he knew she would encourage him and even help him accomplish his dreams. He knew her character was equally as unselfish in her work, fully dedicated and committed.

Eli flinched as Jonah came down the stairs behind him and slapped him on the shoulder.

"You okay, old man? The run didn't hurt you, did it?"

"No. Just thinking," Eli mumbled and watched as Tauri turned and looked into his eyes, the hot pan of croissants still in her mitten covered hand. He saw the anxiety in her expression. Quickly, she looked away.

Jonah was dressed in navy-blue slacks, a blue, red, and green Christmas sweater, and a nice pair of navy lace ups. Eli made eye contact with Jonah and angled his head toward Tauri. Jonah nodded.

"Taur, I took Eli on a running tour of the neighborhood and he kept up, too," Jonah said with a huge grin. "Now I'm ready to party."

He walked over and grabbed a warm croissant from the pan Tauri had placed on the stove top, bit half of it then kissed Tauri on the cheek.

Tauri's eyes grew big.

"Jonah!"

"What? Everything smells so good and I'm hungry!"

"If you would just set the table, we can eat," Tauri said with a frown on her brow.

Jonah frowned.

"Okay, okay. You don't have to get all upset."

He turned and winked at Eli as he walked out of the kitchen.

Jonah had successfully sidetracked Tauri by agitating her like only a younger brother could.

"Is there anything I can do to help?" Eli asked.

Tauri seemed to have a moment of indecision as she looked around the kitchen.

"Yes, please get the pitcher of juice from the refrigerator along with butter and jelly."

After they were seated and the prayer was said, Tauri went over the activities for the day.

"Today, we're going to two parties: one at the senior center and the other at the northern center."

"The northern center has the biggest recreation room," Jonah added.

Tauri continued; "we will probably be at the senior center an hour and a half and the daycare center for about two."

"Yeah, the kids always want to hear 'Twas the Night Before Christmas'," Jonah said.

Tauri laughed at Jonah's exasperated expression.

"Jonah, you don't need to talk. When you were about three all the way through seven years old, mom could not calm you down on Christmas Eve unless you heard that story. So, what's that saying?"

"Don't throw stones when you live in a glass house," Eli quoting the old expression.

Eli and Tauri both laughed.

"After we finish at the northern center," Jonah announced. "I'm going to meet up with some of the guys for eggnog."

"All right, but you know how Aunt Ellie gets when you are late for her Christmas dinner."

"Okay," Jonah grinned. "I promise to be there by midnight."

Tauri looked at the clock. "Well, let's finish up and get going."

After brunch, he and Jonah volunteered to clean Tauri's kitchen. Tauri warned them before she went to get dressed, "make sure it looks the way I always leave it."

Eli and Jonah laughed but neither one of them wanted to disappoint her, so they were careful to follow her instructions.

When she appeared in the foyer, Eli was speechless. He could honestly say he had never seen a more beautiful woman. Tauri looked stunning in a form fitting knee length long sleeved red dress. She wore red tear drop earrings with a matching necklace. Her beaded bracelet held a number of tiny breast cancer ribbons in different shades of pink.

Eli knew it was to show support for the millions of women and men who have suffered—and are suffering from the terrible disease. And he surmised, it was a constant reminder of what she had gone through. For some reason, it felt like a punch in the gut to think of what she had suffered. He wondered if she was fearful it would come back.

All the ladies at the senior center were dressed in their holiday finery. The attire was everything from sequins to ball gowns to ugly sweaters. Eli was again inundated with greetings and hugs. He took the time to chat with each of the women and wished them happy holidays.

Not many family members were present because it was the day before Christmas Eve. The center usually invited friends and family on Christmas Day. Eli noticed Tauri watching him as he circulated through the ladies in the hall. The only reason he noticed was because he was watching her as well.

Tauri turned at the sound of her brother's voice.

"Excuse me ladies. Tauri, may I talk to you for a moment?" She smiled up at Jonah.

"Sure, I'll be right back Miss Mamie."

Miss Mamie nodded and walked off to speak with some of the other ladies.

Jonah guided her into the business center. It held five desk top computers, two writing desks and a large television monitor. Jonah closed the door.

"Have a seat, Tauri."

She frowned.

"What's going on, Jonah?"

Jonah remained standing.

"First, I want to get this out of the way. We've always been straight with each other. I had a hunch when I was in New York that Eli had grown attached to you. When I got back to Chicago he was in a foul mood for days. So, I decided to ask him to come to California to see if I was right."

Tauri's eyes grew wide in surprise.

"Eli is a decent guy, Tauri. He had a bad break-up a few years ago. I saw his previous girl on a few occasions, and she looked really high maintenance. I haven't seen him with anyone else since."

"He was in a foul mood?" Tauri asked with a heart full of hope.

"And so were you, if I recall, right?" Jonah smirked.

"I wasn't that bad," she lied.

"I almost came back early because I was beginning to worry about you." Jonah's frowning demeanor said as much.

She stood and placed her hand on his chin.

"I'm sorry, Jonah. I didn't mean to make you worry about me."

He placed his hand over hers.

"I always worry about you, Sis. I want what is best for you, Tauri and I don't like that you are here all alone, all the time. I was thinking about moving back next year."

"Jonah?"

"But a new opportunity recently arose."

"What new opportunity?"

"Eli has decided to open his own advertising agency and he has asked me to join him."

"What did you say?"

"I said I would talk to you and let him know after the holidays. What do you think?"

She searched her brother's eyes and asked, "what is your heart telling you, Jonah? I wanted you to go out and find yourself, become your own man. I did the best I could to guide you and make sure you had the best education available. Again, and as I have told you before I am very, very proud of you. I am sure mom and dad would be also. I think you are more than capable of making this decision on your own. Whatever the decision is, I'll stand by you."

"Thank you, Sis."

They hugged each other, then stepped back.

"You know I saw you two together this morning."

Tauri looked down.

"Tauri, you are my big sister. I know you have a life and it made my heart glad to see you so peaceful."

"Thank you Jonah," Tauri said hugging him before rejoining the party.

When they arrived at the northern center the parking lot was almost full, so both vehicles were parked on the curb after the toys were unloaded. Eli didn't think he had ever seen so many children under five in one place before. He hoped there were enough toys.

Eli held the door open for Tauri and when she walked into the recreation room, the room exploded into cheers and screams.

"Miss Tauri! Miss Tauri!"

She was instantly surrounded by children, some hugging her, some being hugged by her and some yelling at her to tell them a story.

She was radiant! The smile on her face was so big and bright and genuine, she glowed. Slowly, she went down on her knees.

"I missed you all. Hi, Thomas. You've gotten really tall. Wow!"

Little dark-haired Thomas smiled and tied to stand even taller. Tauri continued until she hugged every single child. As she hugged them, she greeted each one by name. She was so amazing.

Jonah called from the far corner of the room; "anyone want hot dogs and hamburgers?"

The entire herd erupted in screams of, "I do's," as the children ran to find a seat and place their orders. Tauri was laughing as she looked after them. Eli smiled, helping her stand.

"Are they always so excited?"

Tauri straighten her dress when she stood beside Eli.

"It's Christmas and they're kids. There are hot dogs and hamburgers *and* it's Christmas."

"Yeah. To be carefree and that excited."

"I also think the fuel for some of that energy is the tree with all the presents."

"Yes, all that may have something to do with it, but the main reason is you, Tauri."

"Me?" she blushed.

"It's plain to see that those little ones adore you."

"Oh, and I adore them right back. I spend a lot of time with them."

"You make them feel special."

"They are special—each and every one of them."

She thought for a moment.

"While some of them are very young, they already show a lot of promise. If you begin telling them from an early age how very special, and intelligent they are, they will start to believe it and someday change the world."

Eli broadly smiled, "you sound like my mother."

"I do? "

"Yes, she's a retired schoolteacher. She always says to shape a young mind is a very important responsibility. It must be done with care."

"And she's right. It only takes a moment to give encouragement and the same time to tear down. Both parenthood and teaching are the most important jobs in the world. You never know if you are talking to a future leader, an amazing teacher, a mayor, doctor, or a future president."

"You're right."

Jonah made his way back to them.

"Hey, you two! Want a hot dog or hamburger?" He asked as he took a large bite out of his hotdog.

Eli and Tauri both smiled.

"I was about to ask your sister if she would have dinner with me tonight."

Eli and Jonah stared at Tauri. She looked from one to the other as she spoke.

"I ... I need to go to the mall to do some last-minute shopping."

"Great. I need to pick-up a few things as well," Eli replied with a smile on his face.

"Well, okay. That sounds good," Jonah said as he finished his snack. "I suggest the *Citrus City Grille* at Dos Lago. They have a really good menu with a lot of variety."

"So does *The Cheesecake Factory*," Tauri countered.

Jonah wiped his mouth with a napkin.

"True, they do have great food, but the *Grille* has dancing," Jonah yelled, as he walked back to the children. "Who wants presents?"

As expected, cheers went up all over the room. Eli watched as two young girls who looked to be about five, ran over and grabbed Tauri's hands.

"Miss Tauri, come on and give out the presents."

"All right but first, I want to introduce you to someone." All three looked up at Eli.

"Girls, this is Mr. Eli Thornton. Mr. Eli, this is Amani and Cameron. Say Merry Christmas, girls."

Eli thought Tauri and the girls made a beautiful sight. Amani had a big red, white, and green ribbon in her hair matching her dress, and Cameron wore a big red bow in her braided hair to match her red dress.

"Merry Christmas, Mr. Eli," the girls said in unison.

Amani asked, "Are you Miss Tauri's boyfriend?"

Cameron also wanted to know.

"Yes, are you?"

Eli looked to Tauri.

"That's a good question Miss Tauri. Am I your boyfriend?"

Now three sets of eyes were focused on her. Tauri sighed then smiled at Eli.

"Yes. Mr. Eli is my boyfriend."

Eli was smiling, not realizing he was holding his breath until she answered. And his heart soared.

Tauri looked down at Amani and Cameron.

"Okay ladies, let's go get some presents."

Eli shook his head then followed the trio.

Boyfriend!" he said under his breath.

Eli looked on as the teachers helped take presents from under the tree and passed them out. Before long everyone in the room except Eli, Jonah and Tauri had a gift. Just as Jonah had predicted, one of the kids yelled out, "Story, Miss Tauri. Story!"

Then the others joined in the chant.

Tauri made her way to the center of the room. Someone handed her a large pillow, on which she sat. All the children and their wrapped toys sat on the floor in front of her as she began.

"T'was the night before Christmas and all through the house not a creature was stirring, not even a mouse."

The kids were mesmerized, hanging on her every word. The adults in the room were also quiet. The only sound in the room was Tauri's voice and a restless infant.

Eli was also mesmerized by this stubborn woman who had so many amazing talents. Compassion and caring for others came as easily as breathing for her. She did not look the least bit tired and she was glowing. The children were as happy and excited as she was.

He smiled as she imitated a male voice while she called out the names of Santa's reindeer.

"Where's Rudolph?" one of the young boys asked.

A young woman leaned over and whispered to him, "Santa didn't need his bright red nose on this trip."

When Tauri finished, they all clapped and yelled, "Merry Christmas!"

When she was done, Eli helped Tauri to her feet. She then asked the staff to meet her in her office. The parents came by and gave Tauri a hug and said, "Merry Christmas," as they guided their young ones out of the door.

Eli followed Tauri to her office. Upon opening the door, she gasped putting her hands over her mouth. The room was full of gifts, flowers, balloons, and drawings. The teachers gathered behind her and Eli. Tauri turned to face everyone; her eyes filled with tears.

"Thank you, guys. Oh, my goodness, I never expected anything like this!"

Eli grinned as Claire walked up and hugged her.

"You are well loved, Tauri. The children all made you something and the rest is from the staff and parents."

"Thank you!" Tauri said through her tears and all the staff came up and gave her a hug.

Eli gave her some tissue from the box on her desk. Tauri cleared her throat as she turned around and walked over to her desk. She bent over, pulled out the top drawer of her desk retrieving some envelopes.

"I wanted to tell you all what a great job you've done with both centers in the last year," Tauri said. "I could not have done it without you. Thank you so very much for the overtime, the early mornings and for caring about all these little angels. You all know my heart is in these two centers.

"I also wanted to have a place where parents can bring their little ones knowing they would be safe and well cared for while they are at work or school. You have gone above and beyond over, and over again. Thank you!"

"When I did the budget last year, I decided to add a little extra. I wanted to do this last year because you all worked so very hard, but there was nothing left. So, I am especially happy to give all of you a Christmas bonus this year.""

Gasps and mummers sounded around the room.

"It is not much, but it is something," she offered as she gave the stack of envelopes to Claire to hand out as she accepted thanks and more hugs from everyone.

After all the embraces and holiday joy, some of the staff helped Eli load all of Tauri's gifts into the trunk of her car. They then wished them a Merry Christmas and a Happy New Year.

"What a day!" Eli said, as he drove the sedan onto the east bound Interstate 91 freeway. The traffic slowed as they approached the exit to the mall.

"I'm sorry. This exit used to have two lanes. About two years ago someone thought it would be a good idea to have only one," Tauri said as she frowned at the line of cars waiting to get off the same exit.

"It's okay, I'm good. I made our dinner reservations for seven, so we have plenty of time."

"I didn't know we needed reservations."

"Jonah suggested I make reservations because it was so close to Christmas and it's Friday."

Eli smiled, as he inched the sedan down the off ramp.

"My little brother. He still amazes me."

Tauri looked over at Eli as he looked at the slow-moving traffic. He looked at home behind the wheel of her car. She reminded herself that Eli had the same make and model, although it was one year older.

"Jonah told me you asked him to go into business with you."

Eli gave Tauri a glance before answering, "yes, and what do you think about it?"

"I told him I was proud of him and he would have to make the decision on his own."

The traffic moved in front of them. Tauri directed Eli to get in the outside left turning lane. He nodded, then she asked,

"Where are you planning on setting-up shop?"

"I had planned to set it up in Chicago, but now I have to consider Jonah's opinion regarding the location."

Eli made a left at the light, then a right into the parking lot of the *Galleria at Tyler Mall*. The lot was full of vehicles however he was lucky and found an empty spot not too far from the mall entrance.

Tauri waited until Eli came around and opened the car door for her. Reaching for her hand, he helped her out of the car. He was not especially fond of shopping. When it came to holidays or birthdays, he preferred shopping online or made his purchases early.

As they entered the main entrance, Eli was surprised by the number of last-minute shoppers who crowded the mall in front of them.

"Wow!"

Tauri turned to him apologetically.

"I know. I'm sorry, but I only have to go to one place."

She pointed to a mall directory.

"If you know what you're looking for, you may be able to find a store over there."

He frowned and looked at the crowd again.

"Can I just go with you?"

"No," was her quick response.

Tauri almost smiled at the expression on Eli's face. He looked annoyed by the crowd that swarmed around them. She reached up and smoothed the frown from his brow.

"We'll meet back here in an hour. Is that alright?"

Eli looked down at Tauri and placed his hand over hers. He knew she was here to get him a present. He started to tell her his present was just being here with her. He nodded, released her hand, and watched her disappear into the crowd of holiday shoppers. What was he going to do when it was time to go back to Chicago?

Chapter 16

Tauri made it back to their meeting place in the mall in record time with ten minutes to spare. Eli was waiting for her, dangling a big red shopping bag. They hurried to the car since the traffic from the mall was terrible. Tauri suggested he get off the freeway on the Magnolia offramp just two exits from where they entered the freeway. The side streets were almost as slow, but they made it through.

They made it to the *Citrus City Grill* just seven minutes before their reservation time. The hostess showed them to their table on the patio. A jazz trio was playing a cover to Stevie Wonder's 'Superwoman' on the other side of the wooden dance floor.
Although it was a winter night, the air had only a slight chill to it.

"I'm glad you grabbed your wrap," Eli told her. "It may get cooler."

"I'll be okay. I love it," she said smiling. "This time of the year is so special with all the lights and decorations."

Eli took his seat and the hostess placed a menu in front of each of them.

"Enjoy your meal," she said with a smile.

"Thank you," Eli and Tauri answered in unison.

"My pleasure."

When the hostess was gone, Eli noticed there was a tall propane patio heater near Tauri's chair. He motioned to a passing waiter, pointed to the heater and mouthed, "please light the heater."

The waiter nodded and did as Eli requested. Eli focused on Tauri's beautiful face in glow of the overhead light.

"It is a very special season; so special, you can watch '*It's a Wonderful Life*' again," Eli said half-jokingly.

Tauri laughed and answered, "no. I can watch that anytime. It's the season of giving I so love. It's the excitement on the children's faces and the crowds going from here to there buying gifts for their loved ones."

"It's also a lonely time for some," Eli pointed out. "Some people may be experiencing their first Christmas without a loved one or unable to buy presents; especially for their children."

Tauri sighed, "yes, I know. I experienced that when I opened the first center. Some of the moms were afraid they would not be able to pay their bills, let alone buy presents for their children."

"So that's when you started the toy drive."

It was not a question, but a statement.

"Yes. Those mothers, some fathers and young couples sometimes need help. Some need it every day, so whatever the center can provide for them besides childcare, we try to do or get someone else to help them."

Their waiter came to the table.

"Good evening, my name is Jock. What would you two like to drink?"

Tauri spoke first.

"Do you have any wines from the local wineries?"

"No ma'am, but we do have wines from Napa and the Sonoma Valley."

"Thank you, I'll have a hot tea. No caffeine, please."

"Yes ma'am, and you sir?"

"I'll have a glass of your house Riesling."

"Thank you, I'll be right back to take your orders. May I get you any appetizers?"

"What about a salad, Tauri?"

"That sounds good. I'll have a Caesar salad."

"I'll have the Organic Greens with Dijon," Eli said.

"Excellent," Jock said. "I'll bring the drinks out first, then I'll get the starters."

"Thank you." They said again in unison.

There was trio under the patio gazebo playing a cover for, 'Love's Holiday" by Earth, Wind and Fire. There were patrons seated at tables on the lawn and few couples were enjoying the dance floor.

"They're good. Do you come here when you have a chance?"

"Yes. Claire and I have been here a few times, but I didn't know they had live music out here. I'm glad I found out."

Eli exhaled. He didn't want to imagine Tauri coming here to have dinner with another man, especially her ex. What was he thinking? He had never been jealous—it just wasn't who he was.

"Eli, is there something wrong?"

"No. I was just thinking. So what do you suggest?"

She stared at him for a few seconds then looked at her menu.

"The pot roast, grilled salmon and the filet mignon are all delicious. I haven't tried any of the other dishes.

Looking at the menu, Eli said, "I think I'll try the pot roast. What are you having?"

"I think I'll try something new. I'll have the stuffed chicken breast."

Jock came back with their drinks and salads before taking their dinner orders. Tauri was surprised when Eli ordered for her.

"Excellent," Jock said as he took the menus. "I'll get it right out to you."

Again, they thanked him in unison. Jock hurried off to put in their orders.

They made small talk as they ate their salads.

"This is a good salad and I love the weather. Is it always this warm in December?"

Tauri was wearing her wrap. She frowned.

"This is not warm. It has to be at least 65 degrees to be warm."

Eli said, "this is spring in Chicago."

Then he pushed the sleeves of his light pullover sweater up to his elbow. Tauri just shook her head.

"The saying must be true, about your blood thickening when you live in a cooler climate."

"Yes, and that may be why *Miss California* caught the flu after such a short time in the cold."

"What can I say? It rarely gets very cold here. I do remember it being forty-three degrees for a week or so about five years ago, but it was in January. Some years are warmer than others and you will see people wearing shorts. You just never know and yeah, I was not prepared for your Chicago weather. I had no idea what to expect. I've only been to Big Bear a few times after it had snowed, and those trips were for only one or two days at the most."

"Big Bear? How far is that?"

"It's a little over seventy miles from here. It takes about an hour and half to drive and the road is very curvy and steep. It's an uncomfortable one lane going up and one coming down. How did you get used to such cold weather?"

"When you grow up in that kind of weather, it doesn't bother you as much and you just go with it. I've never heard Jonah say whether you had ever been to Chicago before."

She finished her salad, pushed the plate to side of the table and a passing waiter scooped it up.

"Thank you," Tauri told the waiter before addressing Eli's comment. "I hardly had any free time during the early days when I opened the first center. Knowing I would see Jonah at Christmas was alright and I didn't feel so guilty—not visiting. When he first moved, I was tempted to come and help him find a place to live and make sure it was in a good neighborhood.

"I made him load a program on his phone similar to Facetime so I could see him when we talked. Miss Hattie told me to pull back a little and let him breathe. After that I only called him every other week, or I would text him."

"Jonah was your world," Eli concluded. "Train up a child…"

Tauri smiled.

"Yes, I guess you could look at it like that. You know your Bible. He was always a good kid, but the death of our parents hit him very hard."

"I can imagine and yes, my mom also taught Sunday school. Shelia and I were among her students until we became teenagers and moved up."

Jock returned with their entrees and asked, "May I get you anything else at the moment?"

"No, thanks. I think we're good for now," Eli replied.

"Dessert later?"

Tauri laughed, and said, "we'll see. Thank you, Jock."

"My pleasure."

Eli froze and stared at Tauri.

"What?"

"I love the way you laugh."

"Thank you, Eli. Would you like to say grace?"

He lifted his right-hand palm up across table and was pleased when she placed her hand in his and bowed her head. Eli closed his eyes bowing his head as well.

"Thank you, Lord, for your son dying for us. Thank you for this season of giving and this time spent with groups of special people and especially with this special lady."

Squeezing her hand, he continued, "please give her, her heart's desire. Please protect her and keep her healthy and Lord thank you for this food we are about to receive. Bless the cook and the server. In the name of your son, Jesus, we pray."

And they both said, "Amen."

Tauri cleared her throat.

"Thank you, Eli. That was a wonderful prayer."

"You deserve it Tauri and all the best that life has to offer."

As they ate their dinner, a male singer joined the trio and sang three songs. Eli noticed Tauri tapping her feet.

"Do you dance?"

"I used to. Do you?"

He smiled.

"A little."

They both laughed.

The singer announced a break for the band. Then a D.J. stepped up to a turn table in the corner of the stage and requested people come to the dance floor. Eli stretched out his hand to Tauri.

"You want to see what we can do?"

"Sure. I need to dance off this food."

Eli led her to the floor and joined the other dancers as the D.J. played 'Dancing Machine,' an old Jackson Five tune. Eli repeated whatever dance Tauri fell into. When she changed, he changed. They smiled and laughed when he kept up with her every move. When the music changed again, Eli said to Tauri, "Follow me."

He was not surprised when she followed his lead. The music then changed to a line dance song by an artist named Cupid. The dance was the Cupid Shuffle and the crowd went crazy as more dancers rushed to the floor and fell in step with the instructor. By the time the song was over, Eli and Tauri were laughing so hard they fell into each other's arms.

They walked with their arms around each towards their table. Eli asked, "Where did you learn to dance like that?"

"Dance was my minor in college and was my second love."

"Well, I..."

Tauri came to an abrupt halt forcing Eli to stop as well.

Tauri looked up into a face she had hoped not to ever see again. She felt Eli stiffen as she tightened her arm around his waist.

"Hi Tauri. How are you?"

"Oliver...Oh, I'm sorry, *Oscar*. I'm well. How are you?"

"I'm good. You look nice."

"Thank you. This is my boyfriend, Eli Thornton. Eli, this is Oscar Brown."

Eli's right arm was around Tauri's waist and he was not going to release her to shake hands with this b......, so he nodded. He had gotten a clear signal from Tauri to calm down. So, he let her handle the awkward meeting, not knowing how long he could remain silent.

Oscar looked at him nervously. *'Good,'* Eli thought.

Tauri looked from one man to the other. Eli had an impassive expression on his face. In the short time she had gotten to know him, she had seen that expression before and knew she better end this quickly before it got out of hand.

"Are you here visiting your family?"

"Yes, but I'll be leaving on Monday, to go back to Alaska."

"Well, I wish you and your family a Merry Christmas and a Happy New Year."

Eli was satisfied Tauri wanted to be done with this little reunion. The little weasel probably wanted to speak with Tauri alone however she ended it for him.

Oscar looked stunned but he quickly recovered.

"Oh, okay. I will and you two as well. You really do look well, Tauri."

"Thank you, Oscar."

"Good night," Eli said when Oscar lingered for a few seconds. Oscar slowly walked away his head hanging low. He felt Tauri squeeze his waist again. He looked down at her, "What?" Tauri shook her head. "I'm not the one who forgot his name."

She frowned as she looked into Eli's eyes, then burst into laughter.

"I did. Didn't I?"

She laughed louder, quite sure her laugher was over the top, but she felt free, freer than she had felt in years.

All this time she had wondered what she would say or do if she ever saw Oscar again. She had imagined a number of different scenarios but forgetting his name was not one of them.

Eli was amused and when Tauri continued to laugh, he knew she was somehow releasing something that has been inside her for years. When she leaned against him, he stepped in front of her then held her close with both arms and whispered in her ear, "I'm here, Tauri I'm here."

When the laugher subsided, Tauri looked up into Eli's eyes and smiled. Tears ran down her cheeks.

"Oh, my goodness."

She sniffed, then dabbed at her face. Eli guided her over to their table where she grabbed her napkin and blotted her face.

"Are you all right?"

"Yes."

"Would you like to leave?"

"No, no. It's only eight-thirty and I want dessert."

Eli stared at her for a few moments. Just to make sure.

"Okay. Dessert it is."

After dessert, they sat and talked about their dance techniques and how they would have to go on a serious diet after the holidays. But Tauri was quiet on the ride back.

When they got home, she told Eli what time they were to leave for the beach the next morning then wished him good night.

He was tempted to go after her to talk about what happened with Oscar but decided to let it go. It had been a long day and the talk could wait.

Chapter 17

The following morning Tauri and Eli left for the beach just after 10 a.m. Jonah texted Tauri to let her know he had some errands to run before he headed out to the beach, but he had promised to be there no later than six.

Tauri pulled her aunt and uncle's address up on the GPS. The traffic moved sluggishly along I91 West. The day was clear and crisp with a promise of a beautiful California Christmas Eve day. As Eli steered Tauri's sedan through the center of town, he caught a breath-taking view of the snow-covered San Gabriel Mountains to his right.

Tauri looked over at Eli as he stared past her out of the passenger side window.

"Fantastic isn't it?"

Eli smiled at her then turned his eyes back to the slow-moving traffic.

"Yes, it is."

"California is one of the few states where you can go to the mountains to see the snow in the morning, then come down and spend the rest of the day at the beach."

She looked out the window at the mountains.

"Would you like to go up to the snow before you go?"

Eli laughed then shook his head.

"I've had enough snow for a while, thank you very much. Besides, January and February are our heaviest snow fall months in Chicago and I'm not looking forward to it."

Tauri looked straight ahead at the other holiday travelers, her thoughts focused on the day after Christmas when Eli would be going back to his life in Chicago. He would be leaving her. What would she do with the ache that was beginning to grow in her heart?

She closed her eyes and took a deep breath. She would be alright. Just the way she was when Oscar walked out, she got over it. Tauri opened her eyes and looked at Eli's profile. She pushed the sadness away and decided to enjoy the time they had together and to see what would come.

At that moment, Eli reached over and covered her hand with his. She summoned a smile she hoped would look genuine. It looked as though she succeeded because he smiled back then squeezed her hand.

Tauri directed Eli to the three state routes that would take them to their destination. The locals just called them the toll roads. The first was SR 241, which was routed through the Santa Ana Mountains then SR 261 and then SR 133 through the mountains to Laguna Beach.

As Eli maneuvered his way along the curvy two-lane then one lane road. Tauri pressed her head back against the head rest and closed her eyes again.

"You're tired," Eli said.

"A little, it happens every year. I get so excited about the holidays and all the things I planned to do that sometimes I forget to enjoy the season itself."

"I don't know about that. I saw your face at the center when the children opened their gifts and again when the ladies opened theirs. I think you were just as excited as they were."

She laughed, then opened her eyes again.

"They are a mess. Those ladies get the same thing every year, but they all act surprised as if those cookies were the most precious gift they had ever received. But the kids..."

Eli smiled.

"They all love you, Tauri. They know you care enough every year to go through all the trouble to bake those cookies and place them in those little tins just for each of them. How do you keep up with who can have what?"

"Easy, I spoke with the on-sight nutritionist. She showed me each of their dietary charts, it was not too difficult. They can still enjoy treats if I make sure I know who can't have sugar, wheat, gluten, salt and so forth. Believe me, not one of them is shy about telling you what they want or like."

Eli gave her a quick glance. It amazed him how unselfishly Tauri gave to others without a moment of hesitation or regret. She did not look for anything in return—not even their gratitude. He knew she did it straight from her heart.

"They mean a lot to you, don't they?"

Tauri smiled as if she were remembering something pleasant.

"Yes, Jonah and I try to do whatever possible but especially around the holidays. Our mother and grandmother used to volunteer at the home then after my grandmother passed, my grandfather commissioned the center."

"Jonah told me a little bit about the history of the center."

Eli did not elaborate because he wanted to hear the sound of Tauri's voice.

"Our grandmother used to visit the ladies often since she and Miss Mamie were good friends. After a bad fall, Miss Mamie moved into the senior living facility. Her only daughter insisted she move into the assistant living facility to make sure someone was aware of her whereabouts throughout the day. Her daughter and granddaughter visit her several times during the week.

"Mamma—that's what my mom, Jonah and I called my grandmother, started visiting Miss Mamie and some of the other ladies on a regular basis. During those visits, she noticed so many of the others weren't getting many visitors—if any at all.

"People think neglect of the elderly is when they are not taken care of as far as healthcare, food or decent living conditions. There is also the lack of human contact.""

Eli thought the most important part of it all was human compassion. Someone who cared, family, friends, people who are the most important to them.

"Loneliness is harder when you're older," Tauri continued. "You spend your entire life caring for others but when you're older, everyone is too busy to care for you."

Eli chuckled.

"The group I met didn't seem like they had any of those problems."

Tauri laughed also.

"Miss Mamie and Mamma fixed that many years ago. They brought in a stylist who specialized in all types of hair for the ladies and a barber for the men. The shop is open four days a week. There's an exercise program, including water aerobics, a nutritionist and an offsite travel coordinator to help when someone wants to travel or to plan their annual trip to Las Vegas."

"Las Vegas?"

"Yes, fortunately or unfortunately, it is a favorite past-time for the elderly. Some end up spending too much or developing a gambling habit."

"Isn't that taking a chance by encouraging them?"

"Ah, that's where Jonah comes in. A month before their trip, Jonah comes home and meets with the ones who are interested in taking the trip. They all know if they are responsible for paying their monthly expenses, they must have a money order or a cashier's check in hand before they can sign up."

Eli could see Jonah laying down the law to the ladies.

"Does he ever have any troublemakers?"

"Yes, but he's very firm. If they do not have the necessary money, he grounds them. Most of them are on a fixed budget, so many people think when they win a little at the machines, they can double it. Before you know it, they've accessed their checking or saving accounts and are broke until their next allotment."

Eli smiled. "I can see Jonah doing that, but I can also see how the ladies would try to charm him."

"Yes, they do, but Jonah is very stern and stubborn about that subject. If they do not have the money order or cashier's check, they do not go on the trip."

Eli felt good. Their conversation was comfortable and more importantly Tauri *looked* comfortable. During the rest of the trip, Eli admired the scenery as they traveled through the toll roads which were cut through a portion of the Cleveland National Forest.

When Eli rounded the curve leading to Pacific Coast Highway, Laguna Beach and the Pacific Ocean were fully displayed before his eyes.

"Tauri, this place is beautiful," Eli said, with wonder evident in his voice.

"Yes, I know. I come down here all the time and it never ceases to amaze me. There are at least three other ways to get here but this way is the most beautiful."

Eli was so mesmerized as the Pacific Ocean spread out before them, when he stopped at the light at PCH and Laguna Canyon Road, Tauri had to prompt him to make a left when the light turned green.

"How long have your aunt and uncle lived here?"

"About twenty years or so. They have a small condo right on the cliffs overlooking the beach. We'll go down about five blocks then make a right."

As Eli pulled into the bumper to bumper traffic, the navigation system gave him the same instructions. When they arrived at their destination, Eli looked around for nonexistent parking space, Tauri gave him the answer before he asked.

"When I called to let them know we were on our way, my uncle told me he parked on the street and left the parking space open for us. Jonah will have to find one for himself when he arrives."

Eli maneuvered the sedan into the covered space Tauri indicated. He got out and came around the back of the car and opened Tauri's door. She had gotten used to his gallantry and didn't try to dissuade him. Deep down, she actually liked the attention. Eli went to the trunk and retrieved their overnight bags.

They walked up the steps to the door and Tauri rang the bell.

"Be right there," came a deep muffled voice from inside.

When the door swung open, the smell of cinnamon and bayberry rushed out. A tall, well-built man with black and gray close-cropped hair stood in the doorway and glared at Eli. His sharp brown eyes made a quick survey of Eli over the top of a pair of black framed reading glasses.

His eyes lit up when they focused on Tauri. He pulled her into a fierce bear hug.

"Hey, baby girl, it's about time you arrived."

The older man held onto her as if he had not seen her in years. He closed his eyes for a few moments, kissed Tauri on her temple, released her and stepped back, tears glistened in his eyes.

"Oh, Uncle," Tauri sniffed, "look what you've done."

She wiped her eyes with her hands.

"Can't help it, baby girl, I don't know what we'd do if we ever lost you."

He pulled her close and gave her another quick bear hug then kissed her temple again. Unashamed of his show of emotion, he pulled back again and looked at Eli. He faced Eli with his left arm rested loosely around Tauri's shoulder. Tauri was still wiping away tears.

"John Robertson young man."

He offered his right hand.

Eli blinked as he was caught up in the emotion of the moment. He was surprised at how emotional they both still were about something that happened years ago.

Eli realized he was still holding the bags. He set them down then shook hands with John Robertson.

"Elijah Thornton, sir. It's a pleasure to meet you."

John's grip was strong as he held Eli in his assessing gaze.

"Elijah, it's a pleasure to meet you."

"Please call me Eli, sir."

Uncle John nodded.

Tauri looked from one man to the other as again, she wiped tears from her face.

"Uncle John, Eli and Jonah are on the same team at the advertising firm in Chicago. Where's Aunt Ellie?"

"Ellie," John called out. "The kids are here."

Eli could not remember the last time he was called a kid.

"Coming," a cheerful voice replied from somewhere down a small hallway.

Seconds later, an older woman about Tauri's height but quite a bit heavier, came around a potted palm. She paused in the hall when she spotted Tauri.

"Hi, Tauri!" she screamed as her arms opened wide to engulf her niece in a big hug. When she had hugged Tauri and stood back she looked over and frowned at her husband.

"For heaven's sake, John, let go of that young man's hand and quit glaring at him."

John released Eli's hand and Ellie reached up and gave Eli a hug and kissed him on the cheek.

"Welcome! Don't mind him," she said glaring at John. "He's a little overprotective of Tauri. How was your drive?"

Eli was momentarily caught up in the warmth of Aunt Ellie.

"It was beautiful. I've never seen anything like it."

"It did turn out to be another one of God's beautiful days didn't it?"

"Yes ma'am. Nothing like Chicago this time a year."

Ellie gave a soft chuckle and turned to Tauri.

"Oh, I like him, Tauri."

Then she turned to Eli and said, "If you miss it, I'm sure Tauri can find time to take you up in the mountains."

Eli smiled.

"No, thank you, I'm fine. It's supposed to be seventy-five degrees today."

"That's the temperature inland, here it'll be more like sixty-five," Uncle John offered.

"Come here, girl," Aunt Ellie said as she turned to Tauri, "let me look at you."

The two women looked at each other for long time. Aunt Ellie shook her head and tears began to flow before she pulled Tauri into another hug. Aunt Ellie was saying something in Tauri's ear, but Eli could not hear what was said.

Uncle John leaned over and picked up the baggage Eli had placed on the floor.

"Come on young man, I'll show you where to put those. They might be a while."

Eli wondered if they were always this emotional when they saw each other. There was obviously a strong family bond and a family resemblance around the eyes and mouth and, of course, the height.

Eli followed John through a long hallway to a group of rooms. John stopped in front of the first opened door.

"This room is Tauri's room."

Eli walked through the door and placed Tauri's garment and overnight bag on the bed covered with a white comforter. Eli thought the room looked just like Tauri; fresh and lively. The room was decorated in different shades of green with light green walls and curtains framed a set of French doors with a view overlooking the ocean. The queen size bed was draped in dark green and was the focal point of the room.

Then John moved to the next door.

"This is usually Jonah's room, but we'll put him on the sofa in the den."

"I don't mind sleeping on the sofa," Eli said politely.

"No, no, Ellie wants you to sleep in this room so that's where you'll sleep. I don't want her saying I was being mean by making a guest sleep on the sofa."

He looked behind them and motioned to the room across from Tauri's room.

"This is the bathroom and our room is at the end of the hall. Jonah said he would arrive in time for dinner. Did you two have breakfast yet?"

"Yes."

Eli thought there was no better time to clear the air with Tauri's uncle. "Mr. Robertson, I have the best of intentions where Tauri is concerned." John stood, looking at Eli, his expression unreadable. He crossed his arms over his barrel chest but said nothing.

Eli rushed on.

"I have only the highest respect for her and would never do anything to hurt her."

"Go on," John said, a frown on his face.

Eli exhaled.

"She's been through a lot in her life. A lot more than any one person deserves. Tauri's a strong woman but she shouldn't always have to be."

Eli verbalized what had been in his heart since he first saw Tauri in that grocery store, buying soup. He wanted to always be there when Tauri needed someone to lean on. If she ever became sick again, he wanted to be there to take care of her.

Eli focused on the older man again. John dropped his arms as a smile formed on his lips.

"I would say she's more than strong."

He then gave a big laugh and clapped Eli on the shoulder.

"And I believe you're in love with her son. It's looks like you just realized that too."

He laughed again.

"How does she feel about you?"

"She's a little resistant. That bastard, Brown, did a number on her, excuse my language."

John grimaced.

"No need. I've called him worse. I didn't like him from the first time I met him. Didn't look me in the eye."

"He left a really bad taste in her mouth."

"Hers wasn't the only one."

"John what on earth are you doing?" Ellie's soft voice said from the other end of the hallway.

"Nothing honey, me and Eli were just having a little chat. I didn't hurt him or anything."

John and Ellie's entire front room was decorated in Christmas red, green and silver. The tree in the family room was not as big as Tauri's but it was beautiful. Eli and John enjoyed the comforts of the room as Tauri and Ellie were busy in the kitchen.

Tauri and Ellie fixed a light lunch of mixed greens salad with vinaigrette, tuna salad sandwiches, fruit, and lemon cake. During lunch Eli told them about his parents, sister, and life growing up in Springfield.

"I can get these few dishes, sweetie," Aunt Ellie said as she stood to clear the table.

Tauri cleared her throat.

"I don't mind helping you Aunt Ellie."

But Aunt Ellie wouldn't hear of it.

"John will help me. Won't you dear?"

John grunted. Ellie waved her hand at him.

"I already did the prep for dinner, so all I have to do is put the casserole in the oven in about an hour. It's such a beautiful day, why don't you show Eli around the city, Tauri?"

"Are you sure?"

"Yes, I'm sure. Jonah told us he would be here by six. If he's lucky, he'll be able to find a covered meter. Sometimes they do that to a few of the meters. Make sure you take a sweater."

Eli and Tauri had both dressed in jeans and long-sleeved shirts for the trip. Tauri changed into her tennis shoes, grabbed her cap from the peg by the front door and her light jacket. They walked back down the stairs and onto the sidewalk toward the shops and restaurants.

As they walked Tauri adjusted her cap.

"I'm glad I brought this cap. This wind is no joke."

Eli had taken her jacket.

"Do you need this?"

He held up his arm.

"No, not yet, thank you."

"I remember you saying your aunt and uncle lived here for twenty years?"

5"I believe they've owned the condo for about twenty years although for years, it was just a vacation home for them. They knew they wanted to retire at the beach but also realized property would be so expensive by the time they were ready to buy."

"So, twenty years ago they bought it for a really good price and rented it out on a short-term basis. Our dad and Aunt Ellie had not talked to each since their father had passed— probably a total of 30 years between communications. Aunt Ellie was the result of an affair our grandfather had when he had traveled on business. Our grandmother never let him forget it and because of the indiscretion, Aunt Ellie was never welcomed into the family.

"As my dad grew older, my grandfather arranged for them to meet, however, over the years my aunt had been too hurt to have any type of relationship with our dad. My dad tried to keep tabs on her since he was older and felt protective of her."

"When our grandfather died, she did come to the funeral, and that's when he found out she had married Uncle John. She left the service so abruptly he hadn't been able to get any contact information from her. We didn't know where they had moved."

"Jonah found them through social media when I was diagnosed with cancer. They didn't even know mom and dad had passed away."

"Man, that must've been hard."

"Yeah. I don't think Aunt Ellie has forgiven herself for not keeping in contact."

"Yes, she and your dad were not responsible for their dad's actions. They were still family."

"I know. They never had any children so Jonah and I decided we would always spend Christmas here and visit them as much as we can."
"They're good people."
"Yes, they are."

They walked up to the intersection of Pacific Coast Highway and the SR 133. The waves crashed against the shore and had some people running to higher, dry sand to escape getting their feet wet. There were a few brave souls swimming.

Eli pulled out his cell phone and took a selfie of him and Tauri with the Pacific Ocean in the background. Eli grabbed her hand and they crossed PCH at the light and walked through a few of the local shops and art stores.

"Laguna has so many lovely events throughout the year."
"Like?"
"The annual Arts Festival, and Pageant of the Masters."
"I think I've heard of that. People pose recreating a life size famous portrait, right?"
"Yes, it is wonderful and there are amazing art schools here as well," Tauri said while looking at a beautiful painting of marine wildlife. The images looked as if you could reach out and touch them.
"What a great place to go to college."
"Yes, although it is very expensive."
"I'm sure it is. Would you like some yogurt?
"That sounds good."
They purchased yogurt then walked back to the beach and sat on a bench facing the ocean.
"Oh, my goodness, look at that!"
Out on the shore, someone had built a sand replica of a snow man. He was rapidly dissolving rather than melting as the waves slowly made their way to him.
"It's good to have fun. I bet social media is filled with pictures of him already."

"I'm sure by tomorrow there will be a few more."

Eli ate a spoon full of yogurt then looked at Tauri.

"What happened when we arrived? I'm sure that isn't the reception you usually get when you come to visit."

She smiled, looked at the surf, then back at Eli.

"I had an annual mammogram and ultrasound about a month ago and the doctor saw a shadow. I was told before you and Jonah arrived that it was just dense tissue. Aunt Ellie gets worked up sometimes and I go along for the ride."

Eli nodded. They were silent as they ate their yogurt and listened to sounds of the ocean and the people around them. Eli cleared his throat then asked, "Tauri, what was it like to see Oscar again?"

Eli had not mentioned the incident until now.

"I felt free. I had come up with a few scenarios in the event it did happen. It was definitely a possibility since most of his family live in the city and the surrounding areas."

She looked out at the setting sun and thought it breathtakingly beautiful.

"I had said I'd forgiven him. I did it so I could move on, but the test was to actually face him again."

She looked at Eli.

"After last night, I'm good and thank you for letting me handle it."

"Don't thank me. I was hanging on by a thread. If he had said one inappropriate word, he would've been on the floor."

"I believe you."

She knew he was telling the truth and how much he cared for her. He had come out on his vacation to help her and Jonah all week, only complaining when they had gone to the mall.

Although she had introduced Eli as her boyfriend, she was still unsure it would work between them. She was not sure how much time she could get away from the centers to visit Chicago. With the time and energy needed to start his new business, she doubted if he would have much time to visit California.

Forcing those thoughts from her mind, she gave a heavy sigh.

"We'd better get back. Jonah should be here by now."

Just as they threw their empty containers away and started back down the sidewalk, someone beeped. They both looked; it was her brother. They waved and Eli put his arm around her waist.

"How did your Uncle John stay in such great shape?"

"He was an amateur boxer. Did you notice his nose was a little crooked?"

"Remind me never to make him mad."

Dinner was delicious! The lasagna casserole was filled with vegetables instead of meat and it was the best Eli had ever tasted. The five of them played Scrabble. Ellie and John teamed up and put the younger ones to shame. They talked about Christmases past and soon the good nights were said with everyone drifting off to their respective rooms.

Eli unbuttoned his shirt and placed it on the back of the chair by the bed. As he undressed, he could not help but think of Tauri next door, doing the same thing. She was so beautiful tonight in a moss green, long sleeved maxi dress that hugged every one of her curves. A few times he wanted to pull her into his arms and kiss her senseless. As he walked to the shower, he hoped he would get his chance tomorrow.

Tauri lay in her bed, looking through an old Essence magazine her aunt had left in the room. Eli was leaving the day after tomorrow. It may be a while before they would see each other again. She did not think, she just threw the magazine down and grabbed her robe.

The quiet of the house was keeping Eli awake. He lay in the dark, staring at the shadows made by the full moon when he heard a tap on the French doors leading to the balcony. He jumped out of bed, thankful that he had thought to put on his pajama bottoms before lying down. He looked over and saw a silhouette—Tauri's silhouette! Quickly he unlocked the doors and pulled her in.

"What are you doing out there?" he whispered.

"I couldn't sleep," she whispered back. "I...I wanted..."

"You wanted what Tauri?"

"I don't know. I don't know what I'll do when you leave but I don't want to have any regrets."

Eli untied the tie on her robe.

"We can figure it out together."

As Tauri woke up, for a few seconds she didn't know where she was. She looked down and Eli's arm was across her body. She felt... she had to get the right word for it. Happy. That was it, happy.

Eli lay on his side peacefully sleeping. They had spent the most wonderful night together making love. To Tauri, it was the best she ever had. Eli was so caring, so gentle, tenderly in tune to her needs.

He had been in her thoughts ever since she had met him in the grocery store in Chicago. She had not wanted to like him. She had not wanted to need him. He only had two more days and was then going back to Chicago and to his work. A feeling started deep down in her stomach and threatened to spread over her entire body. It was hard to identify it but now she knew what it was. It was fear. Fear of losing him.

Slowly, she eased out of bed and looked around for her clothes. They were nowhere to be found, so she grabbed Eli's shirt instead. She must have made a sound because Eli stirred, then opened his sleepy eyes and smiled at her. Her eyes stung as he reached for her. Tauri tried to make her feet to move but they would not obey. She had to tell her mind that she did not need him. That she did not want him to pull her back into bed and make love to her like she was the best thing he ever had and never wanted to be without.

Tauri tried to make her feet to move but they would not obey. She had to tell her mind that she did not need him. That she did not want him to pull her back into bed and make love to her like she was the best thing he ever had and never wanted to be without.

Eli pulled himself up on one elbow, the sheet slipped down to his waist, her eyes followed.
He frowned.
"Tauri, what's wrong?"
Tauri shook her head.
"I don't think I can do it, Eli. I don't."
"You can't do what?"
Eli threw back the sheet, got out of the bed and stood in front of her. His heart was beating hard inside his chest. He refused to give into the sick feeling trying to settle around his heart.
Tauri was standing in front of the bed wearing only his dress shirt, tears slowly rolling down her face. He wanted to go to her, but his head told him to just stand there. He reached over and grabbed his pajama bottoms from where they had fallen by the bed last night and pulled them on.
"I can't fall in love with you."
Eli relaxed a little, but only a little.
"Why not?"
She wiped her face with the sleeve of his shirt.
"I'm afraid."
"Of me, Tauri?"
"No. I mean yes. I know you wouldn't hurt me on purpose but..."
It finally dawned on Eli what she was afraid of.
He said softly, "I'm not Oscar, Tauri."
More tears slid down her cheeks then her eyes grew stormy with anger.
"Do you know what it was like to be made guardian of a fifteen-year-old when you are only twenty-one? I didn't know who I was or what I wanted. Do you know how hard it was to go to school and work while keeping an eye on a hormonal teenaged

boy, grieving for our parents all at the same time? Only to finally have someone come along and promise you to always be there for you. You breathe a sigh of relief and say 'finally.'"

She wiped her face, but more tears fell as she sobbed into her hands. The bedroom door opened a crack behind her, and Eli saw Jonah, Ellie, and John on the other side. Eli shook his head before Jonah could speak. He mouthed 'it's okay' and the door slowly closed.

Tauri moved her hands, sniffed then continued.

"When Jonah was away at college and doing well, I thought everything was going to be okay. Oscar came along and promised me he would be there forever. It was great for a few years or so and he even asked me to marry him. I thought we should wait a little while since I had just opened the first center and Jonah was moving away after being hired at DHP."

"Then one day I felt a pain in my left breast. I thought it was a part of my monthly cycle because that was the only time, I noticed it hurting. Just as I began the process of opening the second day care center, my doctor's office sent me a reminder for a mammogram."

"I put it off for a few months because I couldn't schedule the time. I finally went in and had it done. The very the same day my doctor's office called and said I needed to come back in for an ultrasound. His office had scheduled it for the next day. Afterwards my doctor told me he had his nurse make me an appointment with a surgeon. By now I was getting a little more than concerned. I called Oscar to ask him to go with me and he did."

She gave Eli a watery smile.

"Oscar picked me up and took me to the appointment. The surgeon said the mammogram and ultrasound both showed a mass in my left breast which needed to be biopsied. Oscar called me every day to see how I was doing. Thinking back, he was distancing himself from me even then."

"The following Monday, I went into to see the surgeon and was told I had cancer. I was floored. I thought, I would get through this—I had Oscar. The doctor explained the surgical procedure and the two options I had: I could have a lumpectomy or a mastectomy. According to what they found, the lumpectomy would mean radiation and or chemo every day for six weeks. There was a twenty percent chance of the cancer returning in five years."

"If it returned, I would then have a mastectomy followed by another round of chemotherapy for six weeks, then radiation treatments for six weeks. If I chose the mastectomy, there would be a ten percent chance of it returning after ten years.

"That was too much for Oscar and said he could not bear it. He couldn't stay with me and watch me go through the uncertainty."

The tears started to flow again.

"When did you tell Jonah?"

She looked down and admitted, "I didn't want to worry him but how could I not tell him? I knew he would be scared and I waited a few days before telling him. I would have given anything not to see the shocked, fearful look on his face."

"Tauri," Eli whispered.

She inhaled, then blew it out heavily and looked back up at him.

"I know. Immediately, Jonah started searching for my aunt or uncle. I was so relieved. Aunt Ellie stayed with me while I was going through the treatments after the surgery. I don't know what I would have done without her and Uncle John."

Eli remembered this time frame because Jonah had been so distracted. He had gone back home to California almost every weekend or whenever he could be spared; never letting on what was happening. Eli's heart hurt for her and he took one step toward her as she went on.

"I had to take care of this on my own. My father had always taught me that I was responsible for myself and to take care of things."

"I'm sure he didn't mean all alone."

"What else could I do, Eli. I *was* alone. Oscar had left me."

Eli took another step.

"I know baby."

"I was so scared. I had always prayed I would live long enough to see Jonah get married and have children. Cancer gave the illusion, that prayer would be not be answered."

A fresh stream of tears rolled down her cheeks.

Eli was standing only a few inches in front of her now.

"But you got through it."

She sniffed, wiped her face with the sleeve of his shirt again, looked up at him and put her hands flat on his chest. "Yes, I did."

Eli placed one arm around her waist and pulled her head to his chest with his free hand.

"You don't ever have to be scared again."

He placed a soft kiss on the top of her head.

"I'll be right here with you."

Tauri gasped and her head snapped up.

"What are you saying, Eli?"

He smiled as he looked at her, sliding his hand down around her waist and pulling her close again. He had felt a strong emotional certainty about her deep in his soul.

"Sweetheart, I knew I was in trouble when Jonah asked me to check on you while he was out of town."

He wiped away her tears.

"When I saw you in that supermarket buying soup, I was a goner."

She put her head on his chest again.

"No, Tauri, look at me."

When she did, he continued.

"At first, I thought you were the most frustrating, stubbornly beautiful woman I had ever met. I fell in love with you when I realized you were fiercely protective of those you loved and cared about, dedicated to what you believed in, strong, self-confident, and encouraging. Your fierce selfless actions reflected your true character.

"I told myself I could live without you when you left Chicago. Your strong insistence you did not want or need me in your life shut the door to any possibilities. However, those thoughts changed after I talked to my mother."

Her eyes grew bigger.

"You talked to your mother about me?"

"Well, sort of. Before leaving for California, I decided to visit my parents and walked in on them making out on the kitchen floor."

Tauri smiled, and said, "oh, how sweet."

"Yeah, I might need counseling later. This was a new development because theirs had not always been a loving relationship. Anyway, she told me in so many words, I needed to go after you and follow my heart"

"She did?"

"Yes, my mom has always been a wise woman. I need to ask this... Do you love me Tauri?

Tears flooded her eyes again and she tried to lower her head. Eli lifted her chin with his hand. Her eyes were closed. "Open your eyes, Tauri."

It was not a request and slowly she opened them.

"I'll repeat the question. Do you love me?"

She began to cry harder as he held his breath. She bobbed her head.

"Yes, Eli. I love you so much my heart feels like it can't hold it all."

The tightness in his stomach left.

"I'm not Oscar and I know you know that. I have been right here with you and Jonah this entire week. I take my responsibilities seriously. When Jonah asked me to look after you, I took it to heart. I tried to leave you alone when you left Chicago, but we've seen how long that lasted."

She smiled again as he continued.

"I want to be with you for the rest of my life. I promise, I will never leave you, Tauri Hill. Marry me."

"Oh, Eli!"

Over her shoulder, Eli noticed the door was open again. There must have been listening ears on the other side of the door.

"Well?" Jonah asked from the doorway with his aunt and uncle standing behind him.

Tauri turned her head and smiled at him then looked back at Eli who still held her very tight in his arms. She gave him a brilliant smile, and answered, "yes. Yes, Eli. I'll marry you."

Eli looked at Jonah.

"What do you say about opening our new company here in California?"

Jonah grinned.

"I say, I already have a location in mind."

Eli laughed, then focused again on Tauri's face.

"Is that okay with you Tauri Hill?"

"I wouldn't have it any other way. Merry Christmas, Eli."

She smiled when his mouth covered her mouth with his and held onto her even tighter.

They did not notice when the door closed behind them.

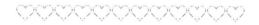

Chapter 18

Eli was laughing so hard at a joke Uncle John had told, he had tears in his eyes. The dinner was outstanding—turkey and ham with all the trimmings. Eli felt at home. They all helped clear the table and put away the leftovers. They'd all agreed to open presents after enjoying dinner.

He and Tauri had called his parents in Florida and his sister in Jamaica that morning after breakfast. Eli's family was surprised and thrilled all at the same time. Eli and Tauri looked forward to visiting his family after the holidays. Sheila and Mitchell had promised to meet them in Florida after the first of the New Year.

Tauri and Jonah both presented Ellie and John with presents. Eli didn't know what to get them, so he bought a bottle of his favorite wine which was served with dinner. He'd already given Jonah a set of cuff links and tie pin engraved with his initials at their office Christmas party.

Tauri bought over a small decorative bag then sat next to him. He removed the item from the bag then unwrapped it. It was a DVD of 'It's a Wonderful Life'. Eli threw back his head and laughed.

"It was to remember me by when you left."

"You do know you can stream the movie online, don't you?" Jonah offered.

"Yeah, but this is better," Eli said, smiling at Tauri.

Eli had put Tauri's gift under the tree before dinner. He stood and retrieved it and handed it to her.

She smiled, "Oh, you didn't have to get me anything."

"Yes, he did," Uncle John's voice boomed.

"John, stay in your lane," Aunt Ellie admonished.

They all laughed.

"You're right, Uncle John. So, open it."

Tauri looked at the silver bag then undid the matching ribbon tie then reached inside. She removed the tissue wrapped object then gasped. Tears immediately flooded her eyes. It was a statue of George Bailey and Mary and the moon. George had a rope in his hands and had lassoed the moon. The caption said, 'I'll lasso the moon for You. Whatever you want.'

"Eli, it's wonderful!"

"Whatever you want Tauri. If I can get it for you it's yours."

She laid her hand on his heart, and told Eli, "I have all I want. I have a heart of trust because of you. I trust you, Elijah Edward Thornton, and I love you with all my heart."

"And that is enough for me, sweetheart."

They sealed it with a kiss.

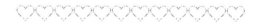

The End

Biography

Carmellia Thorpe-Chavers grew up in Fort Valley, Georgia untill the age of 9 then her family moved 17 miles to Warner Robins, Georgia. As a child she had a very vivid imagination. By the time she graduated high school, she had enlisted in the United States Marine Corps where she served 7 ½ years. When Carmellia read her first romance novel, she was hooked. She started writing in 1996 when she joined Romance Writers of America but 6 Days of Christmas; A Heart of Trust is her first published novel. Her love for romance ranges from sweet romances, to historical, to futuristic, to romantic suspense. It doesn't matter the setting, where there is love anything is possible. Watch out for her next release in mid-2021.

A Message to My Readers

Thank you for going on this journey with Eli Thornton and Tauri Hill. They have been through a lot and will probably go through more. Gratefully, they will now face the future and go through life's adventures together.

I hope you enjoyed reading their story as much as I enjoyed writing it. Now, I think I have to do something about Jonah's story. What do you think?

Carmellia Chavers